David Goodis is the author of
Nightfall, Shoot the Piano Play
filmed), and *The Moon in the*
Street Corner is his 1954 classic.

THE BLONDE ON THE STREET CORNER

David Goodis

MIDNIGHT
CLASSICS

Library of Congress Catalog Card Number: 97–066231

A complete catalogue record for this book can be obtained from the
British Library on request.

First published in the USA by Lion Books, Inc. 1954

First published in this edition in 1997 by Serpent's Tail,
Reprinted 2004
4 Blackstock Mews, London N4

Website: www.serpentstail.com

Phototypeset in 10pt ITC Century by
Intype London Ltd

10 9 8 7 6 5 4 3 2

Printed in Great Britain by
Mackays of Chatham plc, Chatham, Kent

CHAPTER 1

Ralph stood on the corner, leaning against the brick wall of Silver's candy store, telling himself to go home and get some sleep. It was half-past two in the morning and he should have been in bed long ago. The December wind hacked at his face and seemed to slice through his flesh, like saw-toothed blades biting away at his bones. He kept telling himself to go home and slide under a warm quilt. But somehow he couldn't move away from the corner. He was staring at the blonde woman on the other side of the street.

She was wearing a coat of muskrat fur that fitted tight in the waist and emphasized the outward sweep of her wide hips. The coat was somewhat short and it showed her legs with the full calves tapering smoothly to small ankles. She wore high-heeled shoes that propped her up to show the flaunting bulge of her big bosom. She'd been standing there for several minutes, smiling at him and waiting for him to come over and say hello.

He told himself to quit looking at her. She was a married woman who lived here in the neighborhood. That was one thing. Another thing, she was the sister-in-law of one of his close friends. From that point of view, he had no business getting friendly with her. From a deeper point of view, he was afraid of her. There was something about her that caused his brain to sizzle and he was really afraid of her.

He couldn't understand it. She was strictly bargain-counter merchandise. Her type was a dime a dozen. A ripe blonde who used peroxide on her hair and too much lipstick and mascara and walked along the street like she was doing a shake-dance. The sight of her gave him an unclean feeling and he begged himself to quit looking at her. But his eyes remained focused on the big bosom and the narrow waist and the wide hips. On the screen of his mind the fur coat disappeared and he saw her standing there naked.

Just then she raised her arm and beckoned to him. Her thick voice seemed to drift like syrup across the street as she called, "Hey, you."

He didn't reply.

She was putting a cigarette in her mouth. "Hey," she called. "You got a match?"

Mechanically he reached into the pocket of his tattered overcoat. His fingers touched the edge of a match-book. He kept his hand in his pocket as he watched her placing her hands on her hips and shifting her weight onto one leg.

"Well?" she called. It was a dare. It was as though she knew he was afraid.

He took the match-book out of his pocket, pulled himself away from the wall of the candy store, and crossed the pavement to the curb. As he walked slowly across the street, he told himself it didn't mean anything, he was offering her a light for her cigarette, that was all. He promised himself it wouldn't go any further than that.

He came up to her, struck a match, cupped his hand over it, and applied the flame to her cigarette. He was trying not to look at her as she inhaled the smoke. But her greenish eyes were like suction cups that fastened his eyes to her face.

She puffed slowly at the cigarette, took a backward step and looked him up and down. She said, "You need a new overcoat."

"I know."

"Why don't you get one?"

"Can't afford it," he said.

"You that poor?"

"Yeah," he said. "I'm that poor."

Again she looked him up and down. She said, "You'd make a nice appearance if you had some decent clothes."

He didn't say anything.

"What kind of work you do?" she asked.

"I'm unemployed."

She was quiet for some moments, taking long drags at the cigarette. The smoke seeped out of her nostrils and she watched it curling and climbing in a thin column. Her eyes were focused on the column of smoke as she murmured, "Got a girl friend?"

"No."

"How come?"

He shrugged. "It takes cash."

"Not all the time," she said. She leaned her head to the side, giving him the up-and-down look that caused him to squirm. She let the smile build slowly and said, "No reason why you can't have a girl friend. In your case, it wouldn't cost a penny."

He frowned slightly. "How do you figure?"

"You got something," she said. "It's on the special side. I always know when it's on the special side."

The frown deepened. He stood there telling himself to walk away. He couldn't move.

He heard her saying, "You're not like the other bums on the corner. There's something about you that's different. I can't put my finger on it, but I'd sure like to find out."

He tried to switch the frown to a grin. It became a scowl and his voice was tighter than he wanted it to be. "You looking for trouble?"

"I'm looking for something special."

"In what line?"

"A good time."

He didn't know what to say to that. He stood there scowling and blinking and wondering what to say.

She took another long drag at the cigarette. She said, "I'm hungry as hell for a good time. I've been without the real thing for so long, I can hardly remember what it's like. I mean the kind of action that knocks me out, puts me on a roller-coaster going haywire. I'm dying for something like that."

He looked down at the torn leather of his battered shoes. The scowl faded and his face was expressionless as he mumbled, "That's no way to talk."

"Why not?"

"You're a married woman."

"For Christ's sake," she cut in, "let's grow up."

He shook his head. "I don't mess around with married women."

"Oh, for Christ's sake."

"I mean it." He looked at her. His face was expressionless. "I don't play women cheap and I don't let them play me cheap. What I think you better do is go home to your husband."

"That clown?" She snorted. "He can't even give me laughs any more. Only thing he gives me is a stiff pain you know where."

He smiled thinly. "That's your problem."

"Sure it is. But I can't handle it alone." Her tone was matter-of-fact as she added, "Want to help me handle it?"

"No."

"Afraid?"

For some moments he didn't reply. Then he nodded.

"Why?" she murmured. She took a step toward him.

He could feel her breath on his face. It came against him like hot vapor that pushed aside the winter wind. He stared past her and saw the endless line of row-houses that rented for forty-a-month and were assessed at under three thousand. He wasn't sure what his thoughts were, and he scarcely heard himself saying, "I'm fed up with this neighborhood. Damn sick and tired of hanging around on the corner and waiting for something to happen. Gotta get away, that's all. Gotta do something. Find something. Something better than this."

"Better than me?"

He went on staring past her. His eyes remained focused on the sameness of the row-houses that went on and on and finally vanished in the darkness. "There's gotta be something better than this. It can't stay this way all the time, day after day the same loused-up routine, nowhere to go, nothing to do, just standing on the corner and waiting, waiting – "

"For what?"

"Damned if I know."

She took a final drag at the cigarette, flipped it away, and said, "I don't get this line of talk. It's way over my head. I think you been reading fairy-tales, or something. Maybe you're waiting for some dream girl to come along in a coach drawn by six white horses, and she'll pick you up and haul you away to the clouds, where it's all milk and honey and springtime all year around. Maybe that's what you're waiting for. That dream girl."

"Maybe," he murmured. And then he looked at the blonde. His smile was soft and friendly and he said, "I guess that's why I can't start with you. I'm waiting for the dream girl."

She didn't return the smile. She spoke slowly and very quietly. "You'll get started with me. If it ain't tonight, it'll be another night. Sooner or later you'll be tired of waiting, and then it's gonna be you and me."

He winced. He opened his mouth to say something, but

no sound came out. And then it was too late to say anything, because she was walking away. He heard the sound of her high heels clicking on the sidewalk, but somehow it wasn't the sound of departure. It was more on the order of weird cackling laughter coming at him from all sides, telling him he was trapped. He shut his eyes tightly and again the blonde appeared on the screen of his mind and she was naked and she smiled at him and beckoned to him. He told himself he mustn't move toward her. If he did, it would be the loss of his dreams, the end of all hoping for a cleaner better life.

He opened his eyes. He turned and saw the fur-coated figure of the fat blonde halfway down the block on the other side of the street. His mouth shaped a twisted grin and he muttered aloud, "That cheap slob. What do I want with her? She'll never get me."

He put his hands in his overcoat pockets. In one pocket there were a few Indian Nuts that he'd gotten from the penny slot-machine outside Silver's candy store. He popped an Indian Nut into his mouth and chewed contentedly on the shell as he stepped off the curb and started toward home.

CHAPTER 2

Trees with oranges. Big oranges. He reached up to grab one. Then he turned and saw a dog as big as a cow. It was a collie. It was even bigger than a cow. Dogs didn't come that big. He backed away and the dog moved toward him. He was running. The dog bounded after him. He knew he was screaming with fear. But he could not hear himself screaming.

"Ralph, get up! It's almost twelve o'clock!"

He pulled the covers over his head, turned around a few times, experimented to find the most comfortable position. The door opened just as he was pushing himself into sleep once more.

"Get up."

"Ten more minutes."

"I want to do this room. And I want you to get out of the kitchen. Then you're going downtown to get a job."

"Yeah. As if they're waiting for me."

The door slammed shut. For several seconds he kept his eyes closed, and then he was up, out of bed. He stared around at the room. Pale green ceiling, and the plaster was cracked. Burnt-orange wallpaper, and the design was faded to a meaningless blur. A small table. A highboy. A small mirror. A rug in its last stages. A window.

He walked to the window and looked out. Grey winter was freezing itself onto the alley. Narrow alley. The cement was giving way, and so were the outer walls of the dumb-looking plaster houses on the other side.

He walked to the mirror. And he looked at himself.

Gazing back at him, sort of tired and annoyed, was a young man, five feet eight inches tall, weight 153 pounds. The young man was thirty years old and his name was Ralph Creel. He had straight but indifferent light hair and light brown eyes and a straight nose. Once a girl had giggled that he looked like Douglas Fairbanks, Jr. without a moustache. He had told her that she was crazy. But he had not forgotten about it.

As he walked into the bathroom he told himself that one of these days he would get into the habit of getting washed before getting dressed. His mother had been yelling about that for a long time, almost twenty years. But then it was easier to get dressed and then get washed. He shrugged and turned on the cold water.

The bathroom was too small. He had lived in this house for twenty-four years but he would never get used to the bathroom. It was too small. Adeline was always throwing her five-and-dime perfume and face cream and everything around the room and he was always bumping into a bottle or a jar. There would be a crash. His mother would come upstairs and start yelling and he would yell back and later on when his other sister, Evvie, got home from a day of grief behind a lingerie counter there would be another big fight and finally his father would tell them all to shut up. The matter would be ended until another bottle or another jar crashed to the bathroom floor.

He brushed his teeth with a sweet-tasting toothpaste. He swished the foam about in his mouth and then spat it out and scooped water in his palm and drank it fast. It was the one ritual of cleanliness that he actually liked. He liked to keep a clean taste in his mouth.

He gazed at his hands. They looked clean. No need for soap. He held his hands under the cold water faucet. He swished cold water in his face and ran wet hands over his hair. This took about four seconds. Without drying face or hands, he combed his hair in a fraction under six seconds. Then he dabbed a towel at his face, rubbed his hands dry and looked in the mirror. He needed a shave. If he was going in town today to look for a job he would need a shave. But he didn't feel like shaving.

Besides, he didn't feel like going in town today.

He walked into the kitchen. His mother was peeling potatoes. He looked at her. She was forty-eight years old. She looked younger. She did a lot of work and a lot of hollering. She was small and slim and still sort of pretty. She was blonde and she had grey eyes.

"Mom, where's the morning paper?"

"You're not gonna read," she said, without looking up from the potatoes. "You're gonna hurry up with breakfast and get out of the kitchen."

He opened the icebox and took out an orange. He skinned it with his teeth and bit into it. The juice dribbled over his chin. He ran fingers over his chin and said, "Where's the morning paper?" He walked over to the stove and put the light on under the percolator. He said, "I want the morning paper. I gotta see something important."

"In the financial section?"

"Yeah – I'm worried about my stocks and bonds. Where's the paper?"

"In the living room."

He walked into the living room. In a few moments he came back to the kitchen. He said, "It's not in the living room."

"Then I guess Addie took it."

"Oh she did, did she? I guess that's supposed to be smart, taking the paper to work with her. What does she think this is?"

"Who tells you to sleep until twelve?"

"That's aside from the point."

His mother looked up. "It's not aside from the point.

You've got no business getting up so late. Another fellow would get up at seven, or even six, and he would hustle down into town and he would keep going from one place to another, keep looking until he found something. Not like you, you bum. You don't want to work. You never will work. You won't go in town today. I know that. You think I don't know it. You won't go in town today and you won't go tomorrow and the next day. You'll never get a job. You'll never get anywhere. You'll always be a lazy, no-good bum. You and those other no-goods you go around with."

He wasn't paying any attention to her. He sipped black sugarless coffee. Spread before him was the sports page of the *Record*. He was reading about a new lightweight from Southwark, an Italian kid who was supposed to have a good right hand and –

"I don't care if it's digging ditches in the street. I don't care if it's collecting garbage. At least you should be doing something. A man should work. And you're a man – maybe. Anyway, you're thirty years old and in five more years you'll be thirty-five and then what are you gonna do?"

He was deeply involved in the problems that would confront this Italian kid from Southwark. There was a mob of new lightweights hanging around now, and it was the opinion of the sports columnist that the Italian kid would have his hands full with them. The columnist was advising the manager not to rush the kid and –

"Just look at you. You got out of high school twelve years ago. And since then what have you done? Answer me, what have you done? You've done absolutely nothing. Every once in a while Blayner's would call you into their shipping room. You'd make twelve-fifty a week and as soon as things fell off they'd let you go. And why would it be you and not someone else? I'll tell you. I'll tell you sure enough. Because they've got you down pat, mister, just as

I've got you down pat. They know you're lazy. They know you're a clockwatcher. They know you're no good now, and you never were any good and you never will be any good."

This Italian, Nucio, his name was, from Southwark, had knocked out Caesar Thimmons in four rounds at the Olympia. Thimmons was a fast colored boy who had decisioned Johnny Silvo and Jack Haggerty and Mike Phillips. He had been getting the better of the Italian when —

"So what do you do all day? I ask you — what do you do? I'll tell you. You stand on the corner. You stand there with those other no-good bums. The whole lot of you — just standing there on the corner — doing nothing. My God, how can you stand there all day long and not do anything? I'd go crazy, I swear I would."

In the fourth round Thimmons was pounding Nucio all around the ring. His left was working like a charm. He had the Italian against the ropes and he was working the left and then dancing in and flicking both hands to the body. Then it happened. Nucio ducked under a jab and came up with the right and —

"There are so many things a young man can do. I know if I was a young man I'd find something to do. I'd go from house to house selling magazines or dish rags or vacuum cleaners or anything. You eat and you sleep and you stand on the corner and that's all. That's all you do. You and the other bums. One of these days your father is going to get good and fed up with this sort of thing and he'll tell you to get a move on and get a job and bring some money in the house or else. And you know very well what I mean."

Ralph finished his coffee and the article about the Italian lightweight at the same instant. He shoved the paper and the cup to one side and he said, "What are you talking about?"

She stabbed viciously at a potato and said, "You know

very well what I'm talking about. Don't pretend you didn't hear. That's your father's trick. He pretends he don't hear. But he hears every word I'm saying. I'm on to him, all right. And I'm on to you."

"You know, Mom, you're pretty. You don't look a day over thirty-five."

"Now you shut up!"

"Can I have sixteen cents?"

"Sixteen cents?"

"I just thought that you could spare sixteen cents so I could buy a pack of cigarettes."

"Oh you did, did you? Well now, isn't that nice. He wants sixteen cents for a pack of cigarettes. Isn't that perfectly sweet of him?" She took a deep breath. "You ought to be ashamed of yourself – standing there and asking me for sixteen cents for a pack of cigarettes. You look just like a beggar. Standing there and asking for sixteen cents. Ain't you ashamed of yourself?"

"All right, don't give it to me then." He started to leave the kitchen. He took his time.

She said, "For subway fare to go downtown I'd gladly give you the money. You'd be downtown and you'd be looking for a job. But I certainly am not going to give you sixteen cents for cigarettes!" As she said this she took a small purse from the top of the icebox. She reached into the purse and took out sixteen cents.

He reached out for the money. Glaring, she held it away from him.

"Aw come on, Mom – "

"I know I shouldn't give it to you. I just know I shouldn't." She put the money in his hand.

"Thanks, Mom." He smiled at her. She saw gratitude in his eyes. Her baby wanted a pack of cigarettes. And she had given him the sixteen cents. Now he was grateful, his eyes smiling at her. The same light had been in his eyes so long ago in the days when she had held him in her arms, and the milk had dribbled down his chin, and from the sweet pillow of her breast he had looked up at her, and the nourished, contented smile on his face had said, "Thanks, Mom."

CHAPTER 3

They were on the corner. They were leaning against the purple brick wall of the candy store, the three of them. The collars of their coats were turned up, and they kept stamping their feet up and down and blowing into their cupped hands.

"This is not for me," Ken said. "This is definitely not for me." He was thirty-four, a tall, starved-looking creature. He wore a thin topcoat. It was torn. His shoes also were torn.

"What isn't for you?" Dippy said. Dippy was thirty-three years old. One or two or three days a month he helped somebody install oil burners and made himself a few dollars. He was short and thin and he rolled his own cigarettes and plastered his black hair down with a lot of grease. He seldom bathed.

"He means that the cold isn't for him," George said. George was thirty-one. Every election he watched at the polls and made himself five dollars. Sometimes he was a Republican and sometimes he was a Democrat. One election day he got his parties mixed up and wound up in the hospital with a slight concussion and cuts and bruises on the face. He had pale blonde hair, almost white, and his eyes were very pale blue, his skin very pale. He was of medium height and weight and he had strong wrists. At one time he had figured on playing big league baseball. But somehow he never got around to it. He had played third for several sandlot ball clubs in all parts of the city, and he had been kicked off every one of them. Once he had gone down to Richmond, to play in the D league. He lasted one week. He always kept saying that his finesse in fielding was suited only for the big leagues. Finally he said he was disgusted with big league baseball and was definitely through with it. He never wore a hat.

"One of these days," Ken said, "I'm gonna pick me up and head South."

"That's what you said last year," George said, his teeth clacking, his lips bluish.

"One of these days," Ken said, "I'm gonna get on a subway and go downtown and head over to the Baltimore Pike. Then I'll be on my way. I'll hitch straight down to Florida, to Miami. I'll get myself a smart job in some high-class hotel. I bet a bellhop can knock off a clean forty a week down there in the season. I'll live like a duke down there."

"In Florida?" Dippy said.

"Sure. It's the only place in the world. Look how it is up here. A miserable icebox. The wind cuts into you and it's so mean that it makes you mean. D'ja ever notice that? How mean people can be in the wintertime? It's the cold that does it. But down in Florida everybody's happy, and why shouldn't they be? It's warm, it's nice. There's a beach. There's everything."

"In Florida?" Dippy said.

"Sure. I got a good mind to pick me up and shoot down there this week. Why not tomorrow? What's to stop me from starting out tomorrow?"

"I'll go with you," Dippy said.

"Sure," Ken said. "I bet we can make it in four or five days. Now's the best time to go. We'll get bellhop jobs in a hotel and really live."

"We'll go tomorrow, then," Dippy said.

"Sure. We're practically on our way already," Ken said.

George looked at them. He shook his head slowly and then looked at the pavement and sighed.

Ken said, "This is something I been wanting to do for a long time. I been wanting to get out of this lousy town. I gave this town a chance to make good with me. I gave it a good chance. Now I'm through with it, see? I'm through with it for good."

"Now don't do that," George said. "This city'll go to pieces without you."

"I'm not kidding," Ken said. "I'm through. Finished. All done. Tomorrow me and Dippy head South."

"Straight down to Florida," Dippy said.

"That's right," Ken said. He put one hand in the side pocket of his trousers. He pointed a finger at George and went on "I'm not so dumb. I know what's uptown. For six years now I been banging my head against a stone wall, trying to get a song published. You know some of my songs really have stuff. You said so yourself. A lot of people claim I turn out some really fine songs. So what do I do? There's not a single big-time publisher in this city, and I can't send them over to New York because I don't have anybody over there who could push them for me. You see, I don't have an in. I know enough to know that you gotta have somebody to grease things up so it's easy for you to slide in. Listen, I know what it's all about."

"So what's that got to do with Florida?" George said.

"That's what I'm coming to," Ken said. Now he had both hands in the side pockets of his trousers, and his unbuttoned overcoat was pushed back under his arms. "It's this way. You go down to Florida and you get yourself a job in one of these smart hotels –"

"In Florida," Dippy said.

"Yeah, in Florida. Shut up. A guy gets himself one of these jobs, see? Okay, that's the first step. Then he works it smooth. He just takes his time and goes about his job

and he's just another bellhop, see. But now here's where
the real angle fits in. All this time he has his eyes open
and he knows what's going on. So he just takes his time.
He just waits – "

Dippy started to laugh.

Ken was getting angry. "What are you laughing about,
you maniac?" he said. He did not wait for Dippy's expla-
nation. He turned again to George and said, "So here's
what happens. You just take it easy and wait around. And
all this time you're figuring out what's gonna be your best
move. Do you see what I mean?"

"No, I don't see what you mean," George said.

"Aw, what's the use of talking to you?" Ken whined
disgustedly. "You're ignorant, that's all."

"That's a good one," George said. "You're telling me that
I'm ignorant."

Ken said, "Well, Dippy, you making some more phone
calls tonight?"

"Sure," Dippy said.

"How about for Saturday?" Ken said. "Is it fixed up for
Saturday?"

"Sure," Dippy said. "Eats and all."

"One of these days you'll get in trouble with those
phone deals," George said. "We'll come up to the house
and there's gonna be a mob of cops there and we'll end up
in the station house."

"You're not kidding," Ken said.

Dippy said, "What is this?"

George and Ken started to laugh. Dippy didn't laugh.
He never laughed when he said that. It was a sort of
mystic phrase that came from the deepest well in his
mind. When he murmured, "What is this?" he seemed to
be expressing the sum total of all that he had learned
through all the days of his existence. Whenever he said it,
the fellows laughed. Dippy didn't laugh. He never said

it to amuse them. He never explained why he said it, nor
what he meant by it. He just said it, and they laughed,
and they never knew he was not talking to them when he
said it.

George said, "Tell us about this Saturday night affair."

Dippy said, "Last night about eleven o'clock I get home
from the movies. My brother Clarence took me to the
movies. We saw – "

"Never mind what you saw in the movies. What happened with this Saturday night thing?"

"It's eleven o'clock," Dippy said. "My brother Clarence
and his wife and my mother all go to bed."

"Together?" Ken said.

"Aw, shut up," George whined. "Go on, Dippy."

"I'm sitting downstairs alone," Dippy said. "I get hold of
the telephone book and I start to read it. I look through a
lot of names and then I see something that looks nice."

"What do you mean – it looks nice?" Ken said.

"You don't understand," Dippy said. "You're ignorant."
He laughed. "I just look at this name and I know that it's
nice."

"He's a magician," George said.

Dippy went on, "The name is Donahue – Agnes
Donahue. I call her up. She gets on the phone. She asks
me who I am. I say my name is Philip Wilkin. She says
she never heard of anybody by that name. I tell her she
must be crazy. I am an old friend of hers. I say that I used
to live right near her. She asks me where. So then I look
into the phone book again and I see that she lives on the
300 block of Lenner Street. So I make up an address right
near there. And from there on it was simple."

"So what happened?" Ken said.

"I tell her that I was looking through my diary tonight
and I came across something that read like this: 'Today I
met a very fine young lady whose name is Agnes

Donahue. She is pretty. She is charming. Some day I will want to see her again.' Then I explain that the diary is torn and that the date on the page is missing. But it is not the calendar that is important. It is the idea that I must see Agnes Donahue again. She liked that. She started to ask me a lot of questions about myself. I told her that I was very handsome."

George burst out laughing.

"What is this?" Dippy said.

Ken said, "So then what?"

"So then we made the date for Saturday," Dippy said. "There will be eats and all. And four girls, for the three of us and Ralph."

"I don't think Ralph will want to go," Ken said. "He told me that after what happened last week he wasn't going to be in on any of these telephone parties."

"Don't worry," George said. "Ralph will go. Saturday night comes along and he won't have anything to do. He'll go."

"This Agnes is a very pretty girl," Dippy said.

"How do you know?" George said.

"She told me."

"Oh, she told him," George said. "I can see already. This is gonna be good. The last one who told him she was pretty turned out like the cover of an amazing adventures magazine."

Ralph walked up. He went over to the Indian Nut machine and put in a penny. Ken held out his hand and Ralph poured more nuts. Then he walked into the candy store. He came out, opening a pack of cigarettes. He gave one to Dippy and George and he offered one to Ken.

"Thanks," Ken said. "I have my own."

The four of them lit cigarettes.

Ralph said, "I was reading this morning about that

new lightweight from Southwark, that guy Nucio. He's supposed to be good."

"Yeah," George said. "Up the poolroom last night Allie Ferocco was telling me about the guy. Allie says that he's got a good right hand."

"That's gonna help him a lot, I guess," Ken said. "He'll meet up with somebody that's got not only a good right hand, but also a good left. And he'll get his head knocked off and he'll go back to Southwark, driving a truck."

"I don't know about that," Ralph said. "He knocked out that colored guy Thimmons."

"I could take any one of them," Dippy said.

"You?" George said.

They all laughed. Dippy put up his fists and began to dance around George, who laughed and held his sides and then moved in close. Dippy backed away and collided with three empty ice cream cans and four milk bottles that were lined up along the curb. The cans and bottles and Dippy crashed to the street.

Old Silver came running out of the store, yelling, "Whattsa matta, whattsa matta, whattsa matta?"

Nobody could answer. They were all choking with laughter. Dippy got up slowly and brushed melted ice cream from his trousers and glared at Silver and said, "Is that a place to put cans and bottles?"

"Who told you to run into them?" Silver said. "Who told you to make a disturbance?"

"Look at my pants," Dippy said. "Look at my poor pants. Ice cream all over them. My pants are ruined. And my back – I think my back is broken." He reached behind him and touched his spine and nodded emphatically.

"Don't make with jokes," said Silver.

"My back is broken," said Dippy. "Some joke."

"I can't see your broken back," Silver said, "but I can

see three broken milk bottles in the street. You owe me fifteen cents."

"Send me a bill," Dippy said.

Silver shrugged. Then he said, "The least you can do is pick up that broken glass out of the street and put it on the pavement. All I need now is the paper carrier should come and get a flat tire." He went back into his store.

Dippy picked up the pieces of glass, one by one, and put them on the pavement. He looked at the broken glass, and then he looked at his three friends, leaning against the brick wall. He looked at the cold grey sky, and the cold grey walls of the row-houses, and the thin streets, and the branches of thin trees that wavered in slow rhythm.

And Dippy yawned.

CHAPTER 4

Ralph's father worked in an ice plant. He was fifty years old. All his life he had worked with his hands. Now he was tired.

He had thin, straight-combed brown-and-grey hair and light brown eyes, wrinkled at the edges. On the left side of his face was a four-inch scar where a thirty-pound rectangle of ice had crashed into him after sliding off a shelf at the plant. He always wore a dark blue shirt to work and he always carried his lunch in a paper bag. He made sixty dollars a week. He smoked ten-cent cigarettes and he took his wife to the movies at least once a fortnight. They always went to a place that showed double features and gave out free dishes or silverware or something. Norman Creel liked Western movies. He also liked child stars. He was very fond of children.

He walked up the narrow street of row-houses. It was six in the evening. The street had a single lamp-post. The light cut through early winter darkness and flowed along the narrow pavement.

As he approached the light, Creel smiled. He always smiled at the light when he walked up this street after a day's work. The light showed him his way home. It spread a rug of glowing silver across the cold cement, leading to the ninth house from the corner.

He walked up the silver carpet and up the five steps and put his key in the lock and pushed the door inward and he was home. He was tired and hungry and glad to be home, and –

"Who the hell do you think you are, anyway?"

That was Evvie's voice, from the kitchen.

"Shut your big mouth. I don't have to stand for you talking to me like that."

It was Adeline, the younger one. Evvie was twenty-three and Adeline was sixteen.

Evelyn was saying, "Mom, do you know what she did?"

Adeline shouted, "Mom, don't listen to her! She's a liar. Whatever she says she's a liar."

Mrs Creel was hollering, "Both of you shut up! Get out of the kitchen! No – wait – Adeline, I want you to run across the street to the American Store and buy a half pound of those chocolate-covered marshmallow cakes."

"Mom, I don't like those cakes. They taste like glue with sugar – "

"Shut up. They're good cakes. Your father likes them."

"I like Danish pastry," Evvie said.

"She likes Danish pastry," Adeline sneered. "Downtown high society."

"You mind your own business, Mouth," Evelyn said.

"For God's sake will you two shut up already?" Mrs Creel said.

"A half a pound, Mom?" Adeline yelled from the back steps.

"Yes, honey, a half a pound. Now hurry."

Evelyn said, "Mom, honest to God, I'm starved to death. I worked so hard today I thought I'd die. And that dirty rotten louse of a Mayhew – he came over and bawled me out right in front of a whole crowd of customers – "

"My poor baby," the mother said. "I'd like to tell that Mayhew a thing or two."

"Honest, Mom, he's terrible. You know, the conceited type. He thinks he's somebody. He walks around like a general always looking for something to find fault with. So today he don't like the way I've got the slips and panties arranged. And he comes over and talks in that sarcastic way he has. You know, not yelling exactly, but just digging, digging, with that soft, greasy voice he has, like a needle. And all the customers, the dirty slobs – standing there and taking it all in. And Mayhew having the time of his life – you know, because he has an audience, see? So he winds up with this – he says, 'In the future, Miss Creel, please be more careful about the way you arrange your panties.' And then he walks away. So one of the customers starts to laugh. And then another. And then the whole mob of them, the dirty, filthy, vulgar pigs, they were all laughing. And don't think I didn't know what they were laughing at. I know. I'm not as dumb as they think, those slobs. And I know Mayhew said that on purpose. Wise guy. I'll wise guy him one of these days. One of these days he'll make another crack like that and so help me, Mom, so help me, I'll lean across the counter and smack him right across his fresh face. And then, if they fire me, then I'll really let go. I'll tell them a thing or two. And that Mayhew – that rat! Honestly, Mom, sometimes I get so mad I could cry!"

Norman Creel was in the living room, standing at the foot of the stairs, still wearing his overcoat. He was in the front page of the *Bulletin*, reading about a fistfight on the floor of Congress. He came to the line which read, "Continued on page four." He told himself to remember about that, to turn to page four right after dinner. He threw his hat and coat on a chair and walked into the kitchen and said, "Hello, girls."

His wife smiled at him, put her arms about him and kissed him. She was warm from cooking and he held her tightly, and pressed her warmth against him.

Evvie said, "Why, Pop, you old wolf, you!"

Mrs Creel laughed and stepped away so that Evvie could kiss her father.

Creel said, "My two pretty girls."

His wife said, "And what about Addie?"

"That's right – my three pretty girls."

The front door opened and then slammed shut. An instant later there was a knocking. Then the door opened again, and slammed shut again. Addie came tramping through the house, followed by her brother.

Ralph was saying, "Did you have to slam the door in my face? You saw me coming up the steps."

"You're not a cripple. You can open the door for yourself."

"That's not the idea. It's just consideration for other people, that's all."

"Oh, nuts." Addie was in the kitchen, putting the bag of cakes on the table.

Ralph came into the kitchen. He said, "Hello, Pop."

"Hello, son."

The five of them were in the very small kitchen. Mrs Creel turned around to have a look at the soup. Her elbow jabbed into some dishes and she made a frantic grab and just about managed to save them. "Damn it!" she hollered. She put her hands on her hips and looked at everybody and said, "What is this, a convention or something? Come on, out of the kitchen everybody – except you, Evvie. I want to talk to you about those dollar ninety-eight hats you got at the store."

Creel and his son and young daughter trooped through the small breakfast room, into the small living room. The living room had a sofa and two chairs and a small table next to the sofa and a radio. Addie turned on the radio.

The Guy Lombardo number ended and the announcer was talking about a sensational sale at some store. And then he was saying, "For Mary Constantino, for Lucille Demaree, Bobby, Sid, Joe, and the Gang, and Harold, Sissie, Jane, Dolly, and our old friend Josephine Cass –

Cassbo – Cassabolicci – whew! Ha ha ha – don't worry, Josephine, old girl, one of these days I'll really learn how to pronounce your name – ha ha ha – and Fred, Mike and the boys from Olney – we play the Tommy Dorsey record of *When You Awake*."

Soft music glided into the room and drifted from wall to wall.

Addie moaned and murmured, "Oh – it's so – it's so sweet, Ralph. Isn't it a sweet song? Give me part of the paper."

"I'm reading it now."

"Well, you can't have the whole paper – "

Ralph was separating the sports pages from the rest of the second section of the paper. Addie was grabbing and saying, "No, I want this part."

"What part?"

"This part. You can't have it all."

"Damn it, can't you leave me alone? I'm sitting here reading the paper!"

"Well, I want this part," Addie hollered.

"All right, take it, take it." Ralph had to give up the final sport page, which was attached to a feature page carrying four half-page columns entitled Ethical Problems.

Adeline read this feature every night. She read every line of print and sometimes she would cut out something that she wished to keep. This Ethical Problems consisted of letters sent in by young people. The great majority of these letters was sent in by high school girls and concerned problems of a romantic nature, ending with lines such as – "Do readers think I should see this boy any more?

DISGUSTED."

Adeline frowned as she read. Her eyes stared unblinkingly at the Ethical Problems. This was all very serious and had to be studied carefully so a person could use good common sense and come to the right conclusions.

"Sir:

We are two girls living on the same block. Recently a new boy moved into this same block. He is very nice. But he never looks at us. We are both attractive and we cannot understand why he ignores us. What should we do?

PUZZLED."

"Sir:

We are two fellows who can roller-skate as good as any of the so-called 'flashes' from Richmond. We are very good-looking. When we arrive at the rink the girls cluster around us and make a big fuss over us. This is very annoying. Why don't they leave us alone? These girls interfere with our roller-skating. If they don't know how to behave themselves they should be asked to leave the place.

TWO DONS."

Adeline punched at the paper and said, "The very idea! I'd like to tell those smart alecks a thing or two. I'm going right upstairs this minute and write a letter to the *Bulletin*. Who do they think they are, anyway?"

She was breathing hard as she ran up the steps, down the hall and into the bedroom that she shared with her sister. She pulled open the bottom drawer of the bureau, and began to push aside stockings and handkerchiefs and blouses until she found a box of pale green paper and envelopes. The first few pieces of paper were dirty and wrinkled. Adeline's indignation grew and she muttered something about the stationery department in that store on Broad Street.

She began to write furiously –

"Sir:

Who do those TWO DONS think they are, anyway? I go roller-skating with my girl friends and we never pay any attention to the boys, even though they always try to attract our attention by showing off and everything. We can skate just as good as the boys and in fact better. And besides, I would like to take a look at those TWO DONS to see if they are really as good looking as they say they are.

ADELINE."

She read the letter over and nodded emphatically. "I guess that'll tell them," she murmured. Then she addressed the envelope. Before writing her name and address on the rear flap she hesitated. Maybe it wasn't a good idea to let them know her name and address. And on the other hand –

Mrs Creel was yelling, "Dinner's ready!"

In the small breakfast room they all settled down at the small table. They were reaching for food. They were hungry, all of them. They did not talk. They sat there and worked on the food and shoveled it into their mouths. Each was scarcely aware of the others' presence, scarcely aware of the blaring music clattering from the radio in the living room.

All the others were fast eaters, but Creel took his time. His work at the ice plant was enough of a hurry-up process in itself. It slowed all his other activities. It made him eat more slowly, talk more slowly, walk more slowly, think more slowly.

"Norman, take some more," his wife said.

"I got enough here. I'm not finished with this yet."

"Now take some more, Norman. Here – " She put it on his plate.

"Pop, give me the water," Evvie said.

He reached over to hand her the water pitcher.

"Mom, I got an 80 in a history test today," Adeline said.

"That's very nice," the mother said.

And then they were quiet again, eating furiously.

Mrs Creel got up and started to take dishes away. Adeline did the same. They came out of the kitchen carrying plates of vanilla pudding. They all liked vanilla pudding. Three times a week they had it for dessert.

They all leaned low over the table and gobbled up the pudding. Mr Creel took his time with the gobbling. Then they were all drinking water and getting up from the table. The girls stayed to help their mother with the dishes.

Ralph and his father walked into the living room. Ralph lit a cigarette. He said, "Wanna smoke, Pop?"

"No, thanks, son, I got a cigar."

"Cigar? What's the big occasion?"

"One of the boys down at the plant got a good break. Uncle died and left him a lot of money. He's quitting his job. Today he gave all of us cigars." Mr Creel lit up and took a deep, luxurious puff. Exhaling, watching the blue smoke drift up, he murmured, "It's been a long time since I smoked one of these."

Ralph said, "Look, Pop, if that guy's leaving, maybe you can work me in."

The father shook his head. "Couldn't be done," he said. "This fellow's a skilled refrigeration worker. It took him ten years to learn his job."

Mr Creel picked up the paper, started to turn the pages. Ralph sat there, staring at the floor. Whenever he started to talk to his father about jobs, about getting work, about anything connected with work and wages and so forth, the old man would slice the subject, grab the newspaper and end it then and there. He never tried to help Ralph land a job. He never told him about work. Sometimes Ralph thought it was because the old man was disgusted with him. But it didn't seem that way. It just seemed as if his father wasn't interested in the subject. But even then it was funny that he should not want to talk about it. And in a way it was a sort of relief. It was bad enough his mother was always on his ear about getting a job. He was lucky his father just didn't seem to care one way or the other. Sometimes he felt guilty about the matter. He knew that Evvie was giving in ten bucks a week out of her eighteen. He ought to be doing something. But there wasn't anything around. Conditions were bad, that was all there was to it. Could he help it if conditions were bad?

His feet were sprawled out in front, he was sunk deep in the sofa, his hands in the side pockets of his trousers. He glowered at the rug. He turned and looked at his father. His father was reading the paper. He heard the chatter and clatter of his mother and two sisters and the water and the dishes from the kitchen.

Well, he had to find something. Things just couldn't go on this way. He wasn't doing anything now. Not a thing. How could a guy just go on and on – not doing a thing? At least a guy should do something, no matter how small it was. Like his mother kept telling him – anything at all, any kind of a job, so long as it was a job. He could see that now. He could see that in a way he was sort of forced to go out and get something – anything, and for the moment he was promising himself that tomorrow he would be up early and he would go in town.

He crossed his legs at the ankles and took a deep drag at the half-smoked cigarette and then murdered the cigarette in the ashtray. He watched the smoke float from his mouth. He had a good feeling inside. He wasn't a big eater at all but tonight he had been real hungry and he had eaten a lot and now his belly was content. The smoke from the deep drag kept floating from his mouth.

Now he was telling himself that he was really better off than guys with jobs. They were slaves. Sure, he knew. He knew what it was to work in a shipping room and sweat his balls off and listen to the big shots telling him how dumb he was, and pointing here and pointing there, and telling him to do this, and do that, and asking him where he was when the brains were handed out. And the packages, the packages, and the curses, and the paper, the twine. And the dust, the sweat, everybody tired and miserable and muttering curses and hating the boss and hating each other and waiting and hoping and praying for five-thirty to please hurry up and arrive because a guy can stand so much and no more.

And that was a job.

That was what they called "doing something." Well, if that was doing something then he would just sit around and do nothing. If they were dumb enough to stay down there in that hole of a shipping room and die a slow death, he'd just take things easy and hang around on the corner and at least he'd be breathing fresh air. And it didn't make any difference whether the job was in a shipping room or whether it was in a machine shop or a butcher shop or a great big office or where it was. It was a job and it was no good because nothing was good if a guy really didn't get a kick out of doing it. Sure, these fools got a kick out of collecting their pay-check each week, but after all, that was what they were working for, and it was just a question of whether it was worth all the trouble to work and work and work for that check each week, especially when a guy figured out what was on that check. And going even further than that, what were all these guys working for, anyway? The dough? So they spent the dough. What did they spend it on? So if they were single, like him, they had to kick in at least half in the house. If they were lucky to get twenty a week they had to give in ten. That left ten. So what did they do? They had ten bucks in their pocket and they were big men. They spent it on ties and shoes and hats and coats and cigarettes and cokes and in the pool-room and bowling alley and in the taproom, guzzling beer and throwing darts. But most of it they spent on females.

All these fools, these saps, these suckers, with their jobs and the dumb look in their eyes and their clean white shirts with the clean starched collar being wasted on a date with some bag who was using the date to see maybe if this dope wouldn't take her some place where she might meet something worthwhile.

So it would go on and on and on and when Sunday came around the bankroll was zero. Or maybe they had something after all. Maybe they even had something in the bank. Maybe even forty bucks. Pot of gold. Forty bucks in the bank. Now it was really time to settle down. Sure. Thirty bucks a week, forty bucks in the bank. And before they knew what they were doing, these idiots, these fools were actually – now get this – actually – asking the girls to marry them. Did they think they were doing something that would make them happy? That was a good one. Make them happy. Jokes. Why – these fools, these maniacs – they were making the biggest mistake that any man could make. Now they were really going to get hell. Well, it was just too bad for these morons. They had only themselves to blame. They couldn't let well enough alone. They had to go and get married. And now here they were, stuck with something with a big mouth and a face that when a guy took a good look at it, maybe a few months after the wedding, he thought to himself maybe there was something wrong with his eyes. But it wasn't his eyes that needed fixing. It was his brain. And now it was too late.

He was coming home from work – this was good – he was coming home from work, see, and all day long he had nothing but hardship. He was tired and miserable and all he wanted was to be left alone and so he comes home and right away, see, right away she starts in on him. All day long she has nothing to do but figure out reasons for a great big fight when he comes home. So right away she starts and he tells her to shut up. Anyway, he sits down to eat and she don't know how to cook and he wishes he could run over to Broad Street to Horn and Hardart and get something to eat. He won't say anything, though, because he hates to hurt her feelings. So he looks up and what does he see? He sees that face sitting across from him. That face he married. And he wonders what did he do? What in God's name did he do? And he blinks a few times and he even closes his eyes for maybe a few seconds. Maybe when he opens them he'll see that he's back home again, sitting with the family, a single guy again, free to go and come as he pleases and to do whatever the hell he wants to do. But when he opens his eyes he sees it's no nightmare. It's true. Jesus Christ, it's true. That face. And she's yelling at him, yelling about something. That's a good one. As though she has a right to yell. He puts down his knife and fork. Already he's lost his appetite. He's ready for anything because it's up to his neck. She keeps yapping on and on. All of a sudden he lets loose and tells her to shut up or he'll knock all her teeth out. Finally he gets up and goes out and she's crying. And all this they put under the heading of happily ever after. This is what they call wedded bliss.

He laughed aloud. He leaned his head back against the top of the sofa. The laugh rippled as he floated along in languid enjoyment of his thoughts.

His father looked at him and went back to the paper.

Ralph was thinking again about all these married men

with their bliss. And they were still going to work every day. They were still squeezing out that thirty a week and every cent of it, every single cent was being spent. The wives saw to that. The cartoonists, the gag men on the radio made a big joke about it – the wives spending all the money. But it was no joke. There wasn't anything funny about it. It was downright murder. These men were killing themselves for that thirty a week and even if they could save a buck, and they damn well couldn't, their wives made sure that every single cent was spent. But all right – grant that they could save a dollar. So what did they do? What in God's name did they do?

They went and had a baby.

They went and had a baby. Now just figure that out. Just take the time to figure that one out.

He tightened his lips and shook his head from side to side in derision blended with pity.

A baby. And trouble. Trouble and a baby. They made a good team. From the very beginning they made a good team. And then another baby. Hollering all over the house. Trouble. Trouble.

But here his thoughts slipped into a hollow filled with vague greyness. He didn't want to think about it any more. He had a last, misty impression of all these poor fools with their little jobs and little houses and wives and kids and trouble. And he didn't want to think about it any more.

Instead he was thinking of himself.

Thinking of how he was out of a job, and was glad of it. He had it easy. In the mornings he slept as late as he pleased. And he went to bed at whatever time he felt like. And he did whatever he wanted to do. Of course he never had a cent in his pocket, but what difference did that make? No money, no money worries. Except that he knew of a lot of things he would buy if he did have money. His eyes ran up along the worn grey flannel of his trousers. He had paid seventy bucks for this suit, at a time when he had been working. He let the sum caress his mood. Seventy bucks. Seventy solid bucks. Seven hundred dollars. Seven thousand dollars. Seventy thousand dollars. Seven hundred thousand dollars.

He said, "Pop – do you have any loose pennies on you?"

Mr Creel put a hand in his pocket and took out a half dollar, a quarter, and three pennies.

Ralph was looking at the half dollar.

Mr Creel said, "I'd like to give it to you, son, but I'm taking your mother to the movies tonight. Take the quarter and the three pennies."

"Thanks, Pop. I'll just take the three pennies."

"Take the two bits."

"No. Just the three cents."

His father shrugged and gave him the three cents.

Ralph looked starvedly at the quarter as it re-entered his father's pocket. He said, "Treat Mom to a soda after the movies."

His father looked at him, said nothing, only looked, and then picked up the newspaper again.

Ralph started to call himself names. Two bits. He had passed up two bits. He had passed up all the money in the world. It wasn't the first time he had pulled a dumb stunt like this. It wasn't the first time his old man had offered him more than just loose pennies, and he had nixed it.

A quarter. A solid, round quarter. That meant another pack of cigarettes. It meant a coke. It even meant he could be a big man and treat one of his friends to a coke. And he had passed it up.

He looked down at the three cents in his palm. Big deal. Three cents. A penny for Indian Nuts. And the other two cents for loose cigarettes. He didn't like to grub smokes from his friends. Sometimes he had to. Sometimes he even had to grub poison torches that Dippy rolled from a nickel pouch of tobacco. Dippy. He wanted to laugh. Dippy. He thought of the plastered-with-grease hair, and the rags that the guy wore, and the blankness in the guy's eyes, and then he thought of George and Ken, and himself, standing on the corner, outside the candy store. So what? A lot of corners. A lot of candy stores on corners. A lot of guys on the corners outside the candy stores. In this big city a lot of guys on corners. And a lot of big cities in this big country. A lot of corners in all the big cities in the big country. A lot of guys on the corners. A lot of them? Millions of them. Millions of guys on the corners in the big cities. Standing around with their hands in their pockets and waiting for something to happen. What could happen? An earthquake, a flood from a busted sewer, a great big black sedan filled with gangsters being chased by a police squad car, a runaway milk-wagon horse, two kids fighting in the street, a chariot made of solid ivory, drawn by six white horses, and the chariot would be filled with bars of solid gold. And it would come up to the corner where all the guys were standing, and they could just walk over and help themselves to the bars of gold. Then they could go around to the back alley and shoot crap for the bars of gold. Real action there. Instead of starting with a nickel roll they would flip the bars of gold on the cracked cement of the alley and they would have a big play on the first roll. And one of the men would be a big winner. He would have twenty bars of gold, maybe worth about seven hundred thousand dollars. To have seven hundred thousand dollars. Once in a library he had read something that said something about how men with a lot of money spent all that money on clothes and dames and games and travel and everything that had a lot of gloss on it or glitter or glimmer. Glow and gloss and glitter and glimmer, the big men. The big men with the dough and the high grade felt hats and their lavender convertibles with the top down whizzing along a black street in the black night toward a place all lighted up with green and orange and pink and pale blue lights and a circular dance floor that was polished black marble or polished black glass, with a band on a silver bandstand, and nine terrific broads dancing in a straight line and the glitter and the glimmer, the high grade everything that was in this high grade place, the big men talking big, everything big, the glitter, the glimmer, everything big and smooth and high grade. The big men. Big winners. Winners in a great big crap game. Big men, smart men, lucky men. The glitter, the glimmer, the gloss and the glow. And the emerald studs in a white shirt front and seven thousand bucks. Seventy thousand bucks. Seven hundred thousand honest to God dollars. Sing, dice. On the corner, outside the candy store on the corner. On a lot of corners. On a lot of corners in a lot of cities. On the corners of the big cities in this big country. A lot of guys on a lot of corners. A lot of guys standing around with their hands in their pockets and waiting for something to happen in the year of Our Lord, 1936.

CHAPTER 5

It was Saturday night. Dippy was combing his hair. He had black hair and it was thinned. He put a lot of this ten-cent grease on it and plastered it down over his head. He smoothed it with the palm of his hand, kept smoothing it until it was a shiny black cap. He liked the way it looked. He looked at himself in the mirror. He did not smile but he nodded slowly. He looked quite good. He wore a white shirt that had a starched collar. The edges of the collar were frayed. There was a smudge on the collar but nobody would notice that. He wore a green and brown tie. Best of all he wore a suit that his brother had worn only three times. And nobody would notice his torn shoes. Even if they did, his good-looking sleek black hair would make up for that.

In this little row-house he lived with his mother and his brother and his brother's wife. His brother was forty-three and had been married for four years. He was a lawyer and he averaged about fifty a week. His wife was a fat blonde. She had a mouth. She didn't like Dippy. Dippy didn't like her. She didn't like Dippy's mother. Dippy's mother didn't like anybody – except Dippy. She couldn't do enough for Dippy. She was sixty-seven years old. She called Dippy "boy". He called her "toots."

One day Dippy came in the house and saw his mother crying. He asked her what was the matter. She told him she had a feeling that Clarence and his wife would someday go away and leave her alone without anything at all. And Dippy said, "Don't you worry, toots. I'll stay with you. I'll always stay with you." She stopped crying and she held his hand tightly. She said, "You're a good boy." He nodded slowly, unsmiling, and he said, "Sure." He knew that Clarence would not move away, even if the fat blonde wanted to.

All Dippy had to do was to tell Clarence some of the things he had found out about the fat blonde. He knew a lot of things she had done and he knew some of the things she was doing now. He didn't want to say anything to Clarence because he didn't want to hurt his brother's feelings. But if Clarence ever decided to move out and leave his mother with nothing at all, then it would be time for Dippy to say something. He really didn't like the blonde. Her name was Lenore. Once she came into the house while the guys were there and she heard one of them address her brother-in-law as Dippy. Later on she called him that. She said, "Hello there, Dippy." He walked over to her and said, "Don't you call me that. My name is Philip. You can either call me Philip or you can call me Mr Wilkin. But don't call me Dippy." She laughed and said, "But that's what you are, aren't you? You really are dippy, aren't you, Dippy?" He walked across the room and picked up a heavy green glass ashtray. He walked back and held it near her head. He said, "How would you like me to break this over your head?" Her eyes widened, and she stepped away from him. Whenever he remembered that night, he was delighted with the memory.

He turned away from the mirror and looked again at his shoes. He really needed a new pair of shoes. As soon as he got another day's work on an oil burner job he would go out and buy himself a new pair of shoes. Anyway, the least he could do now was to shine those he had on. He leaned over and put his foot on the bed and rubbed his sleeve across one shoe, and then the other. They looked all right.

Before he went into the bathroom he turned to see if anyone was in the front room. When Lenore and Clarence were out on Saturday nights he could sneak in there and pour some of Lenore's perfume on his handkerchief and dab some underneath his collar. He liked the smell of that perfume. He wouldn't be able to use it tonight, though, because Lenore and Clarence had come in and they were in the front room now. They were having a fight. Dippy walked into the bathroom to wash his hands. He had been down in the cellar, fixing the heater, and his hands were black. While he washed his hands he left the door open so he could listen to the fight.

Clarence said, "You bitch, you."

Lenore said, "Don't you call me a bitch, you fat son of a bitch."

"I'll break your head, God damn you. I'll break every bone in your body."

"You lay a hand on me and I'll have you arrested. I'll have you put in jail for the rest of your life, you son of a bitch."

"You fat bitch, you."

"Don't you call me a fat bitch."

"I'll call you what I wanna call you. Don't tell me what to call you. I know what to call you."

"Why you dirty no good son of a bitch."

"Put down that lamp. You'll break it."

Dippy dried his hands and went out of the bathroom and walked downstairs. He looked at the clock. It was eight o'clock. He had to meet his friends on the corner at eight-thirty. He put on his hat and coat and then he stood at the front door and took out his pouch of nickel tobacco and slowly rolled himself a cigarette. He lit up and stood there smoking. He leaned comfortably against the door, smoking and listening to the carryings on from upstairs.

"Put down that lamp."

"Make me."

"Put down that lamp so help me God I'm telling you – "

Dippy took a deep drag at his cigarette. Then he sensed an empty feeling in his stomach and remembered that he had not eaten anything since one o'clock in the afternoon, when he had gotten up and had taken a cup of coffee and a piece of bread. He was always forgetting to eat. If his mother had been around today she would have seen to it that he ate supper. But she was out visiting. She was always visiting neighbors.

He went into the kitchen and opened the icebox. He saw a bottle of milk, half-filled. He uncapped the bottle, put it to his lips and took a few deep gulps. He put the cap back on. What else now? There was hardly anything in the icebox. On a piece of wax paper there were a few slices of cheese. He snapped them into his mouth. He reached deep into the icebox and snatched at a pear that was lost back there. He took two bites and the pear was finished. There was nothing more for him to eat. He closed the icebox and again he was at the sink. He drank a glass of water. Water would fill up the emptiness. He drank another half-glass. Then he walked through the house and when he was at the front door he stopped to roll himself another cigarette. He stood there smoking and listening to the yelling from upstairs.

"You bitch, are you gonna put down that lamp?"

"Make me, you son of a bitch. Make me."

"I'll make. I'll murder you."

"Go ahead and murder me. You'll hang for it. You'll hang by the neck until you are dead."

Dippy took a deep drag at the cigarette and went out and closed the door. He walked down five steps to the pavement. He stood there and looked up at the sky. It was cold, bright blue, with a lot of stars and a full moon. Dippy walked in the direction of the corner candy store.

On the corner they were standing around, eating Indian Nuts and throwing the shells at one another. When Dippy walked up they aimed a barrage of shells at him. He ducked and walked through the barrage and said, "What is this?"

George grinned. "What's the good word for today?"

"Romance," Dippy said.

They all laughed, Dippy the loudest.

CHAPTER 6

Ken went into the candy store to buy a pack of cigarettes. George looked at the pavement. Ralph looked at the sky. Dippy put a penny in the Indian Nut machine and forgot to pull the handle. He stood there waiting for the Indian Nuts to come out. They didn't come out. Dippy frowned at the machine and said, "Come on – come on."

"What's the matter?" George said.

"This machine – I'm getting jerked around." Dippy aimed a punch at the machine. George came over and pulled the handle. Dippy poured nuts into George's hand. He offered some to Ralph.

"Nix," Ralph said. He put his hands in his pockets and slouched against the brick wall.

Ken came out of the store and said, "Let's get going." He gave cigarettes to Ralph and George. Dippy was rolling another cigarette. The four of them walked along the street.

Ralph said, "Where we going?"

"Big party," Dippy said.

"I'm not going," Ralph said.

George looked at him. "Why not?"

"I just don't feel like."

"Eats and all," Dippy said.

"What'll you do otherwise?" Ken said.

"I'll take a walk," Ralph muttered. "I'll go over the poolroom."

"Got any dough?" Ken said.

"I got two cents in my pocket," Ralph muttered.

George said, "What you gonna do over the poolroom with two cents?"

"I'll just sit around. Maybe I can make a loan and hustle a game with someone."

"Yeah, that's a good idea," Ken said. "The last time you were loaned a buck you made a side bet on a game and you had two. And you doubled and worked it up to four. Finally you had ten bucks. So you went out of your head and got into a game with some guy who was just waiting to take the tenner off you. You shouldn't play pool, Ralph. You're snakebitten when it comes to pool."

"Only pool?" Ralph said. His voice was very low.

George said, "What?"

"Nothing," Ralph said. He turned to Dippy and said, "You went and got a date for me, didn't you?"

"Sure," Dippy said. "Dates and eats and all."

"I'm sorry, Dippy. I don't like to let you down, but I – "

"That's all right," Dippy said. "I'll just tell the girl that you fell down a flight of stairs and broke your neck."

George and Ken laughed. Ralph didn't laugh. He felt low. He didn't know exactly why, but he felt very low. He didn't want to go to any party tonight. He didn't want to go anywhere. He didn't want to do anything. He just felt low.

The four of them walked along the street. For almost a full block they were silent. Then Ken laughed and said, "I almost forgot to tell you men. My old man got fifty bucks for that trolley accident."

"No kidding," George said.

"Yeah, they settled today. My old man's walking around like a millionaire. Tonight he slipped me a buck."

"Give it to me," Dippy said.

"I'll give you poison," Ken said. He took change from his pocket and looked at the glinting silver and said, "I haven't had this much dough in my fist for maybe a good six months."

"A single dollar," George said. "A big deal."

They came to the subway entrance. Ralph stayed back. Ken turned and grabbed his arm. "Come on, you jerk."

"What else you gonna do?" George said.

"There's eats and all," Dippy said.

"I just don't feel like doing anything," Ralph muttered.

"What is this?" Dippy said.

"Come on," Ken said, tugging at Ralph's arm. The four of them went into the subway and Ken paid all the fares. He was the money man tonight and he became angry when George wanted to pay his own way. George kept arguing with him. Ralph and Dippy couldn't argue. They didn't have any money.

Standing on the platform, waiting for the subway train, George said, "Why didn't you let me pay my own way? I got twenty cents on me."

"Keep it," Ken said.

"I like to pay my own way."

"Shut up," Ken said.

The train came. They got in. The train was crowded. There were no seats. The train lurched. Dippy nearly fell on the floor.

There was a drunk near the door. He was a big man. He wore work clothes. He had worked hard for a week and now it was Saturday night and he was drunk. He said, "Next stop – Hanker Crossing. Next stop – Hanker Crossing."

"You're wrong," Dippy said. "Next stop is Allegheny Avenue."

A few people laughed. Ken said, "Don't monkey with him. He's got a mean drunk on."

Dippy said, "Next stop – Allegheny."

The drunk looked at Dippy and said, "You telling me what the next stop is?"

"Next stop – Allegheny," Dippy said.

George said, "Cut it out. It's too early at night to start trouble."

"I'm not starting trouble," Dippy said. "The next stop is Allegheny Avenue. Everybody knows that."

The drunk took a step toward Dippy and nearly fell as the train lurched. He growled, "I don't know it."

"Well, you're finding out," Dippy said.

"Yeah?" the drunk said.

"Yeah," Dippy said.

Ken whispered, "Now shut up, Dippy – "

"Listen," the drunk said, "I was born in Hanker Crossing, in Nebraska."

Dippy said, "I don't care if you were born in Salt Lake City."

A lot of people laughed. Ken said to George, "This maniac Dippy is gonna get us in another fight. I know it."

The drunk said, "Next stop is Hanker Crossing."

"Next stop is Allegheny Avenue," Dippy said.

"Are you insulting my home town?" the drunk said. "Are you insulting good ol' Hanker Crossing?"

"I never heard of Hanker Crossing," Dippy said.

"That's an insult!" the drunk roared. "Why, I'll pitch you right through one of these windows."

"I'll bet a hundred dollars you can't do it," Dippy said.

The people were looking at each other and shifting about uneasily. The drunk moved toward Dippy. He was cursing and spitting and his eyes were red and he was mean. Ralph moved toward him and said, "All right, guy – take it easy."

"Who are you?" the drunk said.

"He's a professional fighter," Dippy said.

"I ain't afraid of no professional fighter," the drunk

said. "I ain't afraid of anybody. I'll pitch you and him right out that window together. I'll clean up this whole train. I'll fight every man in this train and every man in this town."

"Don't start anything, guy," Ralph said.

"Oh – no?"

"No." Ralph was getting angry. The guy was drunk, but he knew what he was doing. He was mean and he was showing off.

George said to Dippy, "See? You started something. Now Ralph's getting excited. It's gonna end in a fight. You always have to start something."

Ken whispered in Ralph's ear, "Just ignore him. He's got a real mean drunk on. When a guy's got a mean drunk inside him, he can do a lot of damage."

George said to Ken, "He don't hear you. He's excited now. When he gets excited, nothing can stop him. He's always been that way, since he was a kid."

The drunk said, "I'll take this whole train. Don't think I can't do it. And I'll start with you."

"Come on," Ralph said. "Start with me."

A woman yelled, "Call the conductor!"

Dippy said, "Next stop – Allegheny Avenue."

The drunk shouted an oath. The train lurched. The drunk fell forward and threw big fists at Ralph's face. Ralph took one on the jaw. He took another one in the chest. He couldn't breathe. He closed his eyes and then he opened them fast and saw a fist whizzing toward him. He pulled his head to one side and shot a left to the drunk's stomach. The drunk doubled and Ralph bashed him in the face with a right and a left and another right and another left. Ralph was crazy now and he didn't know what he was doing. He saw the drunk going down but he lifted him with an uppercut and hooked him with the left and he had his right set and quivering, like an arrow, and then men were jumping in to stop the fight. The drunk was on the floor. The train lurched again and everybody was falling over one another and women were yelling. George and Ken were holding Ralph's arms tightly.

Ralph said, "Let me go."

"We'll all get arrested," George said.

The drunk was bleeding from the mouth. He was struggling to break away from the men who held him on the floor. He was shouting oaths and screeching, "Let me up at him! I'll pitch him right through the window!"

"Go on, let him up," Ralph said.

"Call the police station," a woman said.

Ken turned and said, "Aw shut up, lady."

The woman said, "Don't you tell me to shut up, you young hoodlum. You oughta be in jail. I got three sons and I'm a mother."

"That's fine," Dippy said. "I got three mothers."

"You too," the woman said. "You started the whole thing. It's a disgrace."

"Let me at him!" the drunk was yelling.

Ken said, "Let's get the hell out of here."

George pulled Ralph away from all the noise and excitement. The four of them made their way through the crowd and walked into the next car. They kept moving from car to car and then they were in the first car.

Ralph looked at his knuckles. They were skinned. He put fingers to his jaw and said, "Is it swollen?"

"No," Ken said. "You don't have a mark on you."

George looked at Dippy and said, "You fool you."

"What is this?" Dippy said.

Ralph looked at the floor and shook his head slowly. "I didn't want to hit him. He started it. Didn't he start it?"

"Sure," George said. "He had it coming to him."

"I didn't want to hit him. He was drunk. He couldn't fight back," Ralph said. He kept shaking his head slowly.

He was ashamed of himself. He looked up and frowned at Dippy and muttered, "It's all your fault. Why did you have to start with him?" Ralph said.

"I only expressed a point of view," Dippy said.

Ralph looked at the floor. He felt sick. He forgot the burning pain in the knuckles, the throbbing pain in his jaw. He was thinking about the blood coming from the drunk's mouth, and the hurt blended with rage in the drunk's red eyes, and it made him sick and very low and he said, "Let's forget about it."

George and Ken looked at each other. Dippy looked at the advertisement cards above Ralph's head. The subway train screeched as it lanced its way southward through the city.

Four girls sat in a small living room in a small house. They sat waiting.

Agnes Donahue looked at the clock. "They ought to be here soon."

"Maybe they're not coming," Mabel said.

"I wouldn't be surprised," Pauline said.

"I'm expecting the worst," Mabel said.

"Well, what do you want, movie actors?" Agnes snapped. She was twenty-four years old. She was very homely. She was unemployed. She lived here with her widowed mother and her two sisters and her three brothers. Tonight she had chased them out of the house. There had been a terrific fight. Agnes had cried and punched one of her brothers in the eye. The mother had cried. Agnes had screamed that she didn't have any boy friends and now that she had a chance to meet somebody and maybe get married, the goddam family was ruining it for her. The mother and the two sisters and the three brothers had finally walked out of the house.

Mabel said, "I don't think they're coming."

"Oh, shut up," Pauline said. Pauline was tall and very

thin and had buck teeth and freckles. She was twenty-five. She was unemployed.

"I was on Market Street today," Mabel said. "I ate lunch at Kresge's. I had such a delicious lunch." Mabel was twenty-seven. She was short, with a thick waist and thick ankles. Her father had a small grocery store around the corner, and occasionally she helped him. At Girls' High she had been an honor student and she still wore her sterling silver scholastic-honor pin. She said, "And then afterwards I walked up and down on Market Street and you know what?"

Pauline said, "What?"

"I saw Tony Martin coming out of the Earle."

"No!" Agnes cried.

"Yes," Mabel said. "I should die right now if I'm not telling the truth. It was Tony Martin."

Pauline said, "Yes, that's right. He's on the Earle stage this week."

"What does he look like?" Agnes said.

Mabel took a deep breath and looked at the ceiling and shook her head.

"No kidding," Agnes said.

"Well, I'm telling you, he's really something," Mabel said.

"You mean it, kid?" Pauline said.

"Say, listen, I'm not blind," Mabel said.

"Gee whiz," Agnes said.

"His teeth – you ought to see his teeth," Mabel said.

"You got that close?" Agnes said.

"Close?" Mabel sat up straight and her eyes were wide open and so was her mouth. "Why – I was close enough to touch him."

"Did you?" Pauline said.

"You mean touch him?" Mabel was making up her mind

about whether or not to lie about this. She reluctantly decided not to lie.

"Say, what do you think I am, anyway?" Mabel said.

"Well, at least did you get his autograph?" Pauline said.

"I didn't have any pencil and paper, damn it all."

"Tony Martin – gee whiz," Agnes said.

"Yeah," Mabel said, shaking her head hopelessly.

Pauline looked at the clock. "I bet the rats don't show up."

"They'll be here." Agnes looked at her fingernails.

"I can imagine what's gonna come tramping into this house," Mabel said.

"I'm getting nervous," Pauline said. "Suppose they turn out to be a bunch of hooligans."

"So what are they gonna steal?" Agnes said. "There's nothing in this house worth stealing."

"Not even you," Mabel grinned.

"You can go straight to hell," Agnes said, burning.

"Oh, whaddya getting sore about?" Pauline said.

"She's always making remarks," Agnes crackled. "Who does she think she is? She's no Miss America. She ain't got no room to talk."

"Don't be so sensitive," Mabel said.

"You say a lot of things that you shouldn't say, Mabel," said Pauline.

"Don't tell me how to run my life," Mabel said.

They started to argue. They were yelling. They were calling each other a lot of names. The three of them sat there, close together, leaning toward each other and yelling.

The fourth sat alone.

She sat in a far corner of the room, where it was dark.

She felt very low.

Her family had moved to this neighborhood less than two weeks ago. She lived four houses away from Agnes

Donahue. Her father was unemployed and he was hoping to get a job in an auto-body plant. The family had been on relief for a long time. The father was a good welder but the factories in that small town had closed long ago and since then the family had been on relief. Finally the father managed to borrow enough money to bring his wife and children to the big city.

The girl sat in the dark corner of the small living room and thought of her father. She thought of her tired mother. She thought of her kid sister and her little brother. Monday morning she was going to get up real early and go look for a job. She was a high school graduate and maybe she could find something. She had to bring some money into the house. She had to find something. This was a big city and there must be something for her to do and she had to go out and find it. But everything was so new. Everything was so different from what she had known in the little town.

Three days after they had moved into the little house down the street, she was standing outside, getting a bit of air. All morning and well into the afternoon she had been working in the house, working hard, helping her mother to make the place clean. She was very tired and she was standing outside, leaning against the grey brick wall, and looking at two little kids playing on the other side of the street. A girl came up and said hello and introduced herself as Agnes Donahue. She got to talking with Agnes, and then Agnes said it was a shame, not doing anything on a Saturday night, and just moving in like this, to a new city that was so big after living in a small town and all. And Agnes invited her to the big party for Saturday night. At first she hesitated. Then she was thinking that the word party was something new to her. At least, it had been such a long time since she had been to a party, a big party like this was going to be.

She sat there, looking at the big party.

Mabel was saying, "And at least when I borrow something I return it."

Agnes yelled, "Are you making insinuations?"

Mabel said, "Listen, kiddo, you can take it any way you want to."

Agnes screamed, "You can search this house from cellar to roof and if you find that hair curler I'll give you the whole house!"

The girl who sat in the far corner of the small living room was looking at the door. She wanted to get up and go out. She wanted to go home. Maybe her mother was working in the kitchen. Maybe she should be helping her mother. But she remembered her mother telling her that the house was all clean now and she should forget about the house and go to the party and have a good time. A good time at the big party.

She was twenty-three years old. Her hair was a smoky yellow, almost the same color as her eyes. Her skin was soft and clear and clean. But she didn't have any color in her cheeks. She was sort of pale. The only cosmetic she had on was a bit of lipstick. It was more orange than red. And she wore an orange dress. She had made it herself. It was a simple, plain dress, in subdued, simple orange. Her name was Edna Daly.

She sat there, looking at the big party.

Mabel said, "Now don't say things like that, Agnes. You know they're not true."

"Don't you call me a liar," Agnes said.

Edna stared at the torn carpet. She wanted to go home.

The doorbell rang. Agnes got up and hurried to the door. Pauline quickly fixed her hair. Mabel ran her tongue over her lips. The door opened. Agnes was saying hello. She was leading the way into the living room and the four young men followed her. They stood there, looking at the girls. The girls looked back at them. Nobody smiled. Then Dippy said to Agnes, "How are you?"

"I'm fine, thank you," she said.

"I'm sorry to hear it," Dippy said.

His friends laughed. The girls didn't laugh. Agnes frowned and started to burn. She said, "What do you call that, a smart remark?"

"More or less," Dippy said.

Agnes looked Dippy up and down. A disgusted expression flowed over her features. Standing behind Dippy, his friends were laughing.

"What's so funny?" Mabel said.

"Nothing's funny," Ken said. "We're just happy, that's all."

"What do you have to be so happy about?" Pauline said angrily.

Dippy said, "We're happy to be here with all you good-looking girls."

"You wouldn't kid me, would you?" Agnes said.

"I never kid anybody," Dippy said.

Mabel looked at Pauline. And Pauline was looking at Ken. She got up fast and made a beeline for Ken. Mabel followed and started toward George. She tripped over a flap in the rug and fell on her face. Agnes let out a shriek of laughter. Mabel got up very slowly, glaring at Agnes. George helped her to her feet. She turned and smiled at George and said, "Thank you – what is your name?"

"George."

"Thank you, George. My name's Mabel."

They were making introductions, the six of them. The other two were out of it. Edna was staring at the carpet. She wanted to go home. Ralph was leaning against the wall, near the door. He had been standing alone and the girls had not noticed him. He did not look at any of the girls.

"What do you do?" Pauline said. She sat on the sofa. Ken sat beside her, on the arm of the sofa, and lit a cigarette for her.

"I'm a songwriter," he said.

"Oh. You write songs?" Pauline said.

"That's right."

"Gee, that's wonderful."

"What's wonderful about it?" Ken said.

"Writing songs," Pauline said.

Mabel sat in the center of the sofa. George sat beside her. Neither of them said anything. Mabel was thinking that George had real nice blond hair. George wanted Mabel to stand up so he could see what she looked like when she stood up. She looked sort of fat. He didn't mind if a girl was fat as long as she didn't look like a bag. She was soft, anyway. When he had picked her up off the floor his hands were under her arms and she was nice and soft. But if she was a bag he wasn't going to have anything to do with her. He should have taken a good look at her when she was standing up before. He turned his head sideways to get another look at her face and she turned her head toward him and he turned his head away.

Agnes sat in a chair and Dippy stood in front of the chair. Agnes looked Dippy up and down and kept expressing varying degrees of disgust. She looked over at the sofa and glared at Mabel, who had the best-looking one of the lot. This thing in front of her was something that should be either in a museum or a zoo.

"Put on the radio," Dippy said.

Agnes leaned over to the side and switched on the radio. She looked Dippy up and down and said, "Can you dance?"

"I'm a great dancer," Dippy said.

"I can imagine," Agnes said.

Conga music clicked out of the radio. Dippy began to do his version of the Conga. George and Ken burst out laughing. Agnes looked at Mabel. Mabel looked at Pauline.

Agnes said, "What is that supposed to be?"

"This is the Conga," Dippy said. "One – two – three – kick." He kicked with his right foot and his shoe missed Agnes' chin by two inches. She ducked her head away and nearly knocked over a lamp.

"God help us all," she said.

"One – two – three – kick," Dippy said. He kicked again and came within an inch of knocking a few teeth out of Agnes' mouth.

She yelled, "Now you cut that out or there's gonna be trouble."

Mabel said to George, "What's the matter with your friend?"

"He's all right," George said.

Dippy took Agnes by the wrist and said, "Dance with me."

Agnes said, "Jesus Christ – this is awful."

"It could be worse," Dippy said. He resumed his version of the Conga. Agnes stopped and looked him up and down and then he grabbed her again and they were dancing.

"Oh, my God," Agnes said.

Dippy's eyes were half-closed. Always when he danced with a girl his eyes were half-closed. No matter how homely she was, he would half-close his eyes and imagine her to be devastating. He would drift into the stream of the music. He would forget where he was. He would hold her lightly, gently, and gently he would lean his head forward and let his lips touch her cheek, just below her ear –

"Say, what the hell do you think you're doing?" Agnes said, pulling her face away.

Dippy scarcely heard her. Eyes half-closed, he drifted. The Conga had stopped and now the band played a Tango. Soft, languid music, brightened by the click of castanets, and Dippy was in Spain. Soft music of the Tango. A bright green shawl over the shoulder of a señorita. Phillippo Wilkinerino, the great Spanish dancer, was doing a Tango. Wonderful night in Spain.

George and Ken screamed with laughter. Mabel was beginning to see how funny it was. Pauline was half-smiling. She sort of pitied the guy.

"Watch out, damn it," Agnes said. "You're breaking my arm."

"Do the Tango," Dippy said.

"Is that what you're supposed to be doing?" Agnes said.

"The Tango," murmured Dippy, drifting with the wonderful music.

Again he leaned his head forward and again his lips touched Agnes' cheek, just below her ear. She drew her head away and looked at him puzzledly.

"Say, what's the matter with this guy?" she said.

They were all laughing.

Dippy drifted.

Weak light threw a dim glow on the left side of the room. On the right side it was dark. In the darkness Ralph leaned against the wall. He looked at the floor. His eye traced a vague design in the rug, snaking through hazy green, weaving and writhing through loops of hazy grey, and the torn fuzz of the carpet, snaking toward the right. The vague design ended there, where a chair was. A chair, and someone's legs. A girl. He looked at her legs. The shoe on her left foot was torn. Her stocking showed through the jagged gap in the dull black fabric of the shoe. He kept looking at the hole in the shoe. He slouched lower against the wall and looked at the torn shoe and the torn rug. Again his eye traced the vague design, swimming through the green and grey haze. Beyond that there was music and noise and jumping around. A lot of laughing. He didn't want to look at that. He was feeling very low. He looked at the torn shoe again. He turned his head and his eye followed the line of stocking up to the orange of the dress, dim in the darkness, and up the orange of the dress through the vague and colorless darkness to the circle of white there that was the face of a girl who sat in the chair. He half-turned and kept looking at her face. There was nothing in his mind now except the slow-painted portrait of what he saw. And he saw the vague yellow hair, unglowing and plain yellow around the white face, and the plain eyes that were vague yellow, and the plain straight nose and the plain lips that seemed to be orange like the orange of the dress and the white of that face. And the eyes, the yellow eyes that he could see so clearly now because the face was turning and the eyes were looking at him. He was gazing at her and she was gazing back at him and although it was so very dark here in this part of the room, at the same time it seemed to be lit by something that was even brighter than a lamp could ever be, and he was looking at her yellow eyes and he knew that she was looking straight back at him. Neither smiled. He did not know that he was not smiling. He did not know of seconds flowing by as he looked at her. He moved along the wall and then he was standing beside the chair looking down at her. She was looking up at him. He knew now that he had been looking down at her for a long time. He wondered how long he had been looking at her.

He knew that he had to say something and he didn't know what to say. Then he heard her voice. It was low-toned, and soft, and sort of vague.

She said, "Who are you?"

"I'm Ralph Creel."

"I'm Edna Daly," she said.

They looked at each other.

Then he was turning his head away. He didn't want to look at her now. He was afraid to look at her.

He walked across the room and stood in the glow, the weak yellow glow of the lamp beside the sofa. In the center of the room George was dancing with Mabel, and Dippy was dancing with Agnes. The radio blared. A dance band played "Five O'Clock Whistle." The four of them were bumping around out there in the center of the room. On the sofa Ken made observations on life, and Pauline was laughing. The music splashed into the crowded room.

Looking across the room now, his eyes slicing through the light and the jumping dancers and the flicker of shadows bouncing from the walls and falling from the cracked ceiling, Ralph saw the darkness across the room. And in the darkness he saw her again, her orange dress, her face, her yellow eyes looking at him now. He went into the next room and grabbed his hat and coat and started for the front door.

One of the girls said, "Where you going?"

George touched Ralph's arm and said, "Where you going?"

Ralph was putting on his coat and moving toward the door. "I'm getting a pack of cigarettes," he said.

"Your friends have got cigarettes," Agnes said.

Ralph looked at George, and George said quickly, "He smokes his own special brand. He'll be right back."

George and Ken looked at each other and then they looked at the girl who sat alone in the dark corner of the room.

The front door opened and cold air leaped into the room, and then the door slammed shut.

CHAPTER 7

Sunday was grey and cold. There was slush on the streets and slush on the windows. Slush flowed down the windows.

It was cold in the room.

Ralph opened his eyes and looked at the windows. He saw the grey and cold sky and the slush sliding down the glass. He banged his head into the pillow and rolled over. He was tired. He was cold. His toes were freezing. He peered over the edge of the patch quilt. His toes were outside the quilt. He pulled his toes inside. He yawned and rolled over again. He wondered what time it was. He had to take a leak. But he didn't want to get out of bed. It was too cold. He was too tired. But he had to go bad. He cursed a few times and then he counted to five, figuring that on five he would jump out of bed and run to the bathroom and be back in bed before he was fully awake. But at five he was too yellow to get out of bed. He tried again, this time counting to three. Again he stayed in bed. His next try was fifteen, and this time he leaped out of bed and raced to the bathroom and came running back and took a dive into the bed, crawled under the quilt and told himself he was going to stay in bed all day. He wondered why he was so tired. He wondered what time it was. He remembered that he had slept badly. He had been dreaming. What had he been dreaming about? Why wasn't this quilt warmer? A quilt should be real warm. This room was an iceberg. Again he looked up and over the edge of the quilt and saw the opened window. The window ought to be closed now. No wonder it was so cold. The window was wide open. It ought to be closed. How long would it take him to leap out of bed and close the window and get back in bed and fall asleep again? He counted to five. No go. He counted to fifteen. He told himself he wasn't going to get out of bed again, window or no window. He rolled over and wrapped the quilt about him.

The door opened and Evvie's voice said, "Out of bed."

"Get out of here," Ralph said.

"It's one o'clock in the afternoon already. Out of bed!"

"Get the hell out of here," Ralph said.

"Addie and me are doing the upstairs. We're helping Mom. We're not gonna wait for you. We want to get done with this room. You get out of bed or I'll get the cold water."

"You pour cold water on me and I bet I break your head."

From the hall Addie's voice shrilled, "Should I get the cold water, Evvie?"

"I'll murder you! I swear I'll murder the two of you!"

He bored himself into the pillow and wrapped the quilt tightly about himself and groaned a few times.

Addie came into the room with a glass of cold water. Evvie took it and moved toward the bed. She dipped her fingers in the glass and then she sprinkled water on Ralph's head. He squirmed.

"God damn it," he said.

"Get up."

Evvie sprinkled more water. "Get up out of that bed, you bum," she said.

He squirmed again. She sprinkled more water. He threw back the quilt and leaped out of bed.

"Now I'm gonna break your necks," he said. His pajama

pants started to fall down. He pulled them up and tightened them and made a fist at his two sisters.

"Just you lay a hand on me and you'll be sorry the rest of your life," Evvie said.

"Go on, get out of here," he said.

"Hurry up and get dressed," Addie said. "We want to finish with the upstairs."

They went out of the room. Ralph dressed slowly. He looked in the mirror. He looked beat. He ran his fingers along the aged flannel suit. The smooth velvetiness of the flannel was gone and now it was like cotton. He looked out the window, at the grey cold sky and the slush in the alley.

Downstairs he made himself a big glass of orange juice and that was his breakfast. He smoked a cigarette. His mother was in the cellar, fixing things. His father sat in the living room and read the Sunday paper. He asked his father for the sport section. He read about a heavyweight fight out on the coast. He put down the paper and smoked another cigarette. He put on his hat and overcoat and walked out of the house.

He went over to Ken's house, a block away.

Ken was home alone. He was almost always home alone. His parents were always at relatives'. Ken had two brothers and two sisters and they were all married and rented homes or rented rooms of their own. The parents were always visiting the children and Ken was almost always home alone. He didn't get along with his parents. He didn't get along with any of his married brothers or sisters. Home alone, he sat in the small living room, at a broken-down piano, with blank music sheets in front of him and a pencil in his right hand and a cigarette dangling from his lips. Stubs filled a glass ashtray on the piano.

The front door was open. It was always open. Ralph walked in. Ken looked at him and then looked back at the blank music sheet and pecked out a few more notes. Then he swung around on the stool and said, "What happened to you last night?"

"What do you mean?"

"Did you go home?"

"Yes," Ralph said.

"What was the matter?"

"I wanted a pack of cigarettes," Ralph said.

"She walked out a few minutes later," Ken said. "And after that the party got a little wild."

"Dippy?"

Ken nodded.

"What did he do?"

"He did everything," Ken said. "But here's the payoff. He says he's going into the kitchen to get a glass of water. So he goes in and we hear him moving around in there and all of a sudden there's a terrible crash. Honest to God I thought he got killed. We come running in there and we see Dippy on the floor, and a chair is overturned and Dippy has a towel to his head and it's all red and the blood is running down in gallons over Dippy's head."

"Blood?" Ralph said.

Ken started to laugh. "That's what we thought it was. But it was really ketchup. He poured ketchup all over himself and then threw the chair up in the air. It came down with a big noise and so we thought he fell down and busted his head. You should of seen him. The girls were scared to death."

"Poor Dippy."

"Mabel fainted."

"You kidding?"

"So help me God she fainted dead away. She went out cold, stretched out on the floor and it was no joke. Just then Agnes sees the ketchup bottle on the sink and she figures that Dippy is pulling a phoney, so what does she do? She grabs the bottle and she starts to scream. She points to Mabel and she yells that Mabel is dead and then she – " he doubled up with choking laughter and burst out, " – she whacks the bottle over Dippy's head – "

"What's funny about that?" Ralph said. "Did she hurt him?"

"She laid his head open!" Ken shrieked, and then fell on the floor, convulsed.

"I can't see what's funny about that," Ralph said. "Did you take him to a hospital?"

"Wait a minute. Wait till I tell you what happened. Dippy's bleeding. It's not a big cut. But his head's laid open. He falls down and this time Agnes thinks she really killed him or something. Honest, it was murder. In the middle of all the excitement, with Agnes screaming like a lunatic and George and me putting ice on Dippy's head, who should come walking into the house but this Agnes' mother and a whole train-load of kids. Well, that was the wind-up."

"Where's Dippy now?"

"Oh, he's home. He's all right. You can't hurt that guy. You should have seen him coming home in the subway. He made a speech in the subway. He told everybody that he was hit in the head while saving the life of the mayor when a truck ran out of control near City Hall. You should have heard him. So finally we get him home and George stayed there last night."

"Let's go over there," Ralph said.

"All right, wait a minute. I just want to finish this idea." Ken swung around on the stool and lit another cigarette and leaned close to the music he had written. He pecked out a few more notes and then he shook his head. He put down the pencil. He muttered and hummed and hit a few chords and then he started to play his song.

"What's that?" Ralph said.

"Just an idea," Ken murmured. He hit a few more chords, banged hard on the first few bars of the song. "I gotta develop it."

"It sounds funny."

"It's not funny," Ken said, becoming angry.

"Don't get sore," Ralph said. "It just sounds that way to me."

"Listen to this," Ken said. He went on with the song. Half-way through, he broke off and went back to the beginning. Again he swung around on the stool. His voice was low as he said, "Listen – I want you to listen to this. I want you to tell me just what you feel when you hear it. Just keep your mind on it and listen carefully."

He banged his preliminary chords and then the music was slow and he was digging into the song. Ralph stood at the side of the piano and looked at the floor. Music crawled around the room. It slipped down a hill of sound and slowly made its way back again and when it reached the summit it slipped once more. And it kept slipping, trying to gain a foothold but slipping nonetheless and going down and down and down and finally cracking hard and spreading out and dying.

Ken sat there, his arms limp at his sides.

Ralph looked at the floor.

Ken said, "I've got something here. I know I've got something. Just the rough idea, but I'm going to develop it." He was talking to himself. He looked up and he said, "Well?"

"I'll think up some lyrics."

"The lyrics are unimportant. You can do them when I finish working on the tune. I got something here. I know it. At this time of year all the big shots are down in Florida. I'll take these tunes with me so the right people can hear them. That's the only way. That's the only way a guy can get anywhere. He's gotta know somebody. He's gotta have an in. What's the use of kidding myself? No matter how good a guy is, if he doesn't have an in he's up the creek. I'm gonna finish this tune and I'm going down there and get in with the big boys." He was muttering now. He turned around on the stool and his long fingers jabbed at the keys again. And he was playing his song again, soft now, and his voice writhed among the notes as they climbed, and slipped, down and down and down, slipped down. His voice, slipping down with the slipping melody, "When I was a kid my old lady figured that one day I would be a great pianist. I remember when I was nine years old I started taking lessons and the guy told her I had a lot of talent and she put out six bits a week for me to learn the piano." The music, slipping down, trying to grab at something but slipping. He said, "I liked it. At first. I could sit at the piano for hours. I didn't like the scale exercises. It used to be that I would stop looking at the notes and get my own ideas and play that way. It got so I didn't want to take any more lessons and I didn't want to look at the notes. I wanted to use my own ideas. I started to write songs. I wrote a lot of songs. I tore them up, all of them. I'm glad I tore them up. They really weren't any good. If I do it, it's got to be good. If it's not good I'll tear it up. I only want to put out songs that are really good. This one I know is good." He banged hard on the keys, and his voice rose. Then the next chord was subdued, and his voice faded with the chord, slipping down, and he was saying, "But what's the use? Even if it's good I've got to fake my way in. And even then – what will happen? Nothing. What's the use? You do something good, you eat your heart out trying to make it as good as you know how, and then you gotta be a phony to put it across. You gotta grease your way in with the big guys. Then even after that – what happens? What happens to you? After you take something right out of yourself, right out of your insides, and you put it in a song, and you sweat blood making it as good as you know how, and then you shine their shoes and manage to get them to listen to it, maybe you make a couple of dimes. That is, if you're especially lucky."

His forefinger wearily rippled the keys, and the song was ended.

He sat there, staring at the keys.

Ralph said, "You're going to work on it some more?"

"Sure. I'm going to work on it until I've got it just the way I want it. Then you go to work on the lyrics."

They walked out of the house, into the grey cold. It was raining again, and the rain was turning to snow. Slush was on the street. Rain and clusters of half-frozen rain dripped from the trees.

They arrived at Dippy's house. The front door was open. There was a light in the breakfast room. They could hear George laughing. They walked into the breakfast room. Dippy was on the phone. He had a strip of adhesive on his forehead. He was leaning over the phone table in deep concentration.

From upstairs there came the clatter of women's voices.

"What's that?" Ralph said.

"Dippy's old lady and his sister-in-law are having a fight. It's been going on all morning," George said.

Dippy turned from the phone. A feminine voice cricketed at the other end of the wire. Dippy smiled at Ralph and pointed at the adhesive on his forehead. Then he turned, and into the phone he said, "You mean you can't arrange it for tonight?"

He listened attentively to the answer and then he banged the receiver down.

"What did she say?" George said.

"She can't arrange it for tonight," Dippy said.

"Why'd you bang the receiver down?" Ken said.

Dippy shrugged. "I didn't have anything more to say."

"Well, couldn't you at least say good-bye?" Ken said.

Dippy picked up the telephone book and turned pages. "Saying good-bye is a waste of time. I'll call that number again on Tuesday night. That's what I'll do. She'll make a party for us for Saturday night. I'll have another party on Thursday. I'll have a party tonight. I'm just trying to find this number in South Philly. I got a date for myself for tomorrow night. I got one for Wednesday night and maybe I'll have one for Tuesday. That leaves me open for Friday. Friday I'm open for ideas."

George said, "He's got a date every night this week." He turned to Dippy. "You must be in the bucks to have a date every night this week. Let's see your bankroll."

Dippy put a hand in his pocket and took out thirty-seven cents. They all smiled.

"This will see me through," Dippy said. "Of course, if my finances don't hold out I'll have to break the dates. But this cash will be sufficient. I'll only spend carfare one way."

"How will you get home?" Ken said.

"The girl will lend me money. I'm honest."

The guys laughed.

Dippy turned the pages of the telephone book.

Upstairs the yelling was louder.

"Listen to them," George said.

Ken laughed. "What's it about this time?"

Dippy turned the pages of the telephone book. "I don't know," he said. "I never know what it's about."

"Let's go in the living room where we can hear better," Ken said.

George and Ken walked into the living room.

Ralph stood by the table, watching Dippy turn the pages on the telephone book. Dippy was having trouble finding the number. He ran his finger down more names.

"This telephone book is very poor," he said. "There's no system to it. Everything should have a system. That's the way I work when I put in an oil burner. I work with a system. I'm an engineer. That's what I really am. I'm a system engineer. Don't call me a plain ordinary oil burner man. I'm a system engineer." He concentrated deeply on the telephone book and ran his finger down the names and kept turning pages and saying, "The trouble with this telephone book is that it has no system. I can tell that because I'm a system engineer. What is this? I'm going to call up the telephone company and tell them how to make a telephone book that has a system."

Upstairs Dippy's mother said, "You dirty rotten fat slob you. You dirty bum."

"You know what you can do," Lenore said.

"Yes, I know what I can do," the old woman said. "And I know what you'd like me to do. You'd like me to drop dead. Here and now."

"You catch on fast, dearie," Lenore said.

"All right, I'll die for you. Soon I'll die. I'll shrivel up and they'll put me in a coffin. They'll nail up the coffin and they'll put me in the earth. They'll put me down deep in the mud with the worms. You'll like that."

"I'll be tickled," Lenore said.

"With the worms in the mud," Mrs Wilkin said. "Deep down there. But I'll get out. I'll come back. I'll come back and I'll come into your room at night. I'll stand beside your bed. I'll reach down – "

"Don't look at me like that! God damn you, you witch! That's what you are, a witch – "

Something crashed against a wall. George and Ken ran up the steps and down the hall and into the front room. Mrs Wilkin and Lenore were wrestling on the floor. Mrs Wilkin was on top. She had one hand pressed on Lenore's throat and her other hand was a fist and she was punching Lenore in the face. Lenore was screaming and trying to bring up her knee to kick Mrs Wilkin in the groin. And she was reaching up with her fingernails and raking her nails down Mrs Wilkin's face. A broken vase lay on the floor. George and Ken rushed forward and pulled the women apart. Just as they got Mrs Wilkin away, Lenore pistoned her left foot out and kicked the old woman in the breast. The old woman gasped and then gurgled and sagged. Ken had hold of Lenore and she was trying to twist away from him to get at Mrs Wilkin. He had to grab her tight around the middle and she was twisting and writhing and screaming, cursing and spitting. She leaned her head down fast and bit Ken on the wrist. He let out a yell and his hand snapped away. Lenore twisted from him and lunged at Mrs Wilkin, who sagged in Ken's arms.

"Get her away!" Ken yelled.

George reached out and grabbed Lenore by her thick blond hair. He pulled hard and she screeched and whirled and kicked at him and tried to reach his face with her fingernails.

"You better cut that out," George said.

Lenore screeched again and came closer to George and speared her fingernails. One of the fingernails ripped at George's cheek. He stepped back and put a hand to his cheek and it came away bloody. He stared at the blood on his hand. Lenore leaped at him again, spearing with her fingernails. George's hand closed to a fist and he flicked it out and it cracked into Lenore's chin and she sailed across the room and fell over a chair and landed on her back. Her feet were up in the air and her dress was up and she was falling all over herself trying to rise. Finally she plopped down and rolled over on her face and started to sob.

George had a puzzled look on his face. He said, "I didn't want to hit her."

Mrs Wilkin, sagging in Ken's arms, looked at Lenore and smiled contentedly.

Ken said, "We gotta help Mrs Wilkin."

"I'm all right," the old woman said.

George looked at her. "Are you sure?"

"I'm all right. You can go downstairs now. I'll be all right." She put her hands to her breast and pain ran over her face. She walked to the door and there she turned. Again she looked at Lenore and again she smiled. Lenore was still sobbing on the floor. The old woman turned and walked from the room. She walked down the hall, to her own room, and she closed the door.

George and Ken looked at each other.

"Jesus Christ Almighty," George said.

They walked to the head of the stairs. In the front room Lenore had stopped sobbing. She had picked herself off the floor and now she stood in front of the dresser and fixed her hair. George and Ken stood looking at her. Then they heard sounds coming from the old woman's room. Moans.

"Maybe we ought to get a doctor," Ken whispered.

"No," George said. "She's not in pain. Listen."

They listened to the moans of despair coming from the old woman's room. They looked at the closed door and then they turned and slowly walked downstairs. They sat down and Ken took out a pack of cigarettes. They sat smoking and looking at the wall on the opposite side of the room.

The breakfast-room door was closed. Dippy had closed it so he should not be annoyed by the carryings-on from upstairs.

Ralph scarcely heard the noise. He leaned against the side of the breakfast table and gazed through the window. He saw the grey wetness on the grey back-porches of the houses across the alley and above that the grey sky.

Dippy ran his finger along the names and said, "This telephone book has no system." He turned and looked at Ralph. He looked at the closed telephone book. He started to open it. He closed it again. He looked at Ralph and he said, "Do you want her address?"

"What?"

"Her address – do you want it?"

"Whose address? What are you talking about?"

"The girl."

"What girl?" Ralph said.

Dippy said, "The girl from last night. The girl who was sitting there alone in the corner."

"Why should I want her address?" Ralph said.

"I just thought you might want it," Dippy said. "I saw you looking at her. She was looking at you. I thought you might want her address. I asked Agnes. She told me that the girl lived seven houses down the street."

Ralph looked at Dippy, whose eyes were blank. For a few seconds Ralph said nothing. Then he muttered, "What made you think I would want her address?"

"I don't know," Dippy said. He picked up the telephone book once more. He opened it and began turning pages. He touched a forefinger to the tip of his tongue and ran one finger down the names in the pages. He said, "The trouble with these telephone books is that they have no system at all."

CHAPTER 8

Ralph was in his room upstairs, looking at the sheet of paper, the scribbling, the crossed-out words and the words that remained.

He hummed the tune and the words fitted in, flowing. These were the right words. No other words could fit the tune. He folded the paper and put it in his pocket and went downstairs.

Evvie was saying, "That Mayhew. He thinks he's smart. Today – you know what he did?"

Mr Creel tried to sink back into his newspaper. Ralph said, "You're always talking about this guy Mayhew."

"Mind your own business."

"All right."

"You haven't any room to talk – about anybody or anything."

"I wouldn't say that."

"Well, I would. You keep your ideas to yourself. If I was a no-good bum, at least I wouldn't go around criticizing other people. You don't know Mayhew. You don't know what I have to put up with. I work like a slave. But I couldn't talk to you about work. You don't know what the word means. You're a lazy bum, a dirty lazy rotten good-for-nothing bum."

Mr Creel put down the paper. "Now, Evvie, that's not right."

"It is right," Evvie said. "Someone in this house has to tell the smart guy where he gets off. It's high time he gave something in the house."

Mr Creel said, "All right, Evvie, that's enough."

"Let her talk, Pop," Ralph said. "I'm not listening to her."

Addie came in from the kitchen and said. "What's all the noise?"

"Look, High School, go upstairs and do your arithmetic," Evvie said.

"You know what you can do," Adeline shouted.

"Please, please," Mr Creel said.

Evvie turned to Ralph and said, "You ought to be ashamed of yourself, you bum."

"Stop picking on him, Big Mouth," Addie said.

Ralph leaned against the side of the sofa and reached for the sports section of the paper.

Mrs Creel came in from the kitchen, wiping her hands on a towel.

Evvie said, "Mom, don't you think this no-good loafer should go out and get himself a job?"

Mr Creel said, "Cut it out, Evvie."

"I won't cut it out," Evvie declared. "I'm sick and tired of working like a slave in a department store basement."

"Oh, now, please," Mr Creel said.

"If he was any kind of a man he'd go out and get himself a job," Evvie said, looking Ralph up and down and crinkling her face in disgust.

"He's tried," Mr Creel said. "There's nothing around, that's all. Leave the boy alone."

Ralph was reading about a new lightweight from Wilkes-Barre, who was going to fight at the Cambria in a few nights.

"Well, if he can't find a job, let him do something else," Evvie said. "Let him join the Navy."

"Oh, my God, no," Mrs Creel said.

"What's the matter with the Navy?" Evvie said.

"Nothing, but – " Mrs Creel faltered. She gulped hard,

and then she moved toward Ralph, pushed her hand through his hair. He continued to read about the Wilkes-Barre lightweight. Mrs Creel gave his head a playful push and then ran her hand through his hair again and said, "I can just picture this one in the Navy. I think it would kill him. Isn't that right, Ralph?"

Reading about the Wilkes-Barre lightweight's snappy footwork, Ralph nodded.

"It would do him good," Evvie said.

Ralph read about the lightweight's eleven straight wins, with nine knockouts.

Addie went upstairs to do her lessons.

Mr Creel read about a police raid on a taproom down on Arch Street.

Evvie glanced at her fingernails, made a face as she saw that she had too much polish on one of them. The polish was chipped.

Mrs Creel gave Ralph's head another pat and then she walked back into the kitchen.

Evvie picked up a movie magazine and went upstairs to the bathroom.

Ralph started to re-read the article concerning the Wilkes-Barre lightweight. This boy had a lot of stuff. He was very fast and although he had a habit of warning his opponent before throwing a right, it was a fault that could very easily be ironed out. The boy was a comer.

Ralph thought of the young guy, twenty-four years old, climbing into the ring with all the lights and all the yells and the announcer's booming voice. Then moving in and dancing around and pumping a left or two and taking one and giving one and giving another and taking his time and then edging in with a left lead and another left and another left and another left and then the right and watching the other guy fall down, flat on his back, his arms spread wide, out like a light. Good feeling. Sort of a tingle running up and down in the guy. Listening to the yelling crowd, and knowing that the next fight would be bigger, the next even bigger, and going up and up and up. That sort of thing was worth all the work and the trouble and the sweat. Crowd yelling. All the lights. Articles and pictures in the paper. And the bucks coming in. A lot of bucks. The real glitter. It was the sort of thing that might happen to any guy who was willing to gamble.

It was a big gamble. The boy might get rocked with a right some night and go to sleep and it would put him right back where he had started, with the fourth-raters. But that was the gamble. It was that way with a lot of things.

With Ken and himself and their song-writing. For years and years they had been writing the songs, not making a cent, sitting there at the piano and banging away and turning out the tunes. All that time spent was a gamble. The number might come up and then again it might not. But before the dice stopped rolling there was a certain glow inside. Thinking that maybe the number might come up and then again it might not. Maybe and maybe and maybe and maybe not. But so long as there was the maybe there was the glow. It couldn't be that way with someone who worked in a shipping room, or at a bookkeeper's table. Guys like the Wilkes-Barre lightweight, guys like Ken, at least they reached for the glitter. Maybe they would never grab hold of it. But at least they could see it up there, dangling. That was something.

He started to whistle Ken's tune.

He stood up, walked to the front door, put his hand on the knob while wriggling into his overcoat. Then he searched in his pockets, and didn't find a cent. He looked at the floor.

His father was saying, "Come in here. I'll give you some change."

"It's all right," Ralph said.

"Come in here."

He walked into the living room. His father gave him seventeen cents.

Outside, he hurried toward the corner. There was no other place to go.

George and Ken and Dippy arrived on the corner. They were arguing. Ralph listened for a few minutes and then joined in the argument. It had to do with a certain shot in billiards.

The billiard argument fizzled to a stalemate. Then Ralph talked about the Wilkes-Barre lightweight. George and Ken got in another argument, concerning the middle-weight situation. Dippy told about a few phone calls he had just made. George spoke about how he had gone in town again today and found exactly nothing. He said, "You ought to see the crowds on Market Street. You oughta see them all. I bet there was a million people in town today. You might think that something special was happening. But it's just another day. And there they were, in town, going up and down and up and down on Market Street. What are they all in town for?"

"Whaddya mean, what are they in town for?" Ken said, anxious for another argument.

"They just don't come in town to walk up and down, do they?"

"Listen to this dumb jerk," Ken said. "Tell me, you had a reason for going in town today, didn't you?"

"Sure. I went in town to look for a job."

"All right, so maybe a lot of them were there for the same reason. Or they were going into stores to buy things. Do you think people are crazy? Do you think they come in town, from all parts of the city, just to walk up and down on Market Street?"

"Do you know what I think?" George murmured, looking at the curb.

"What do you think, George?" Dippy said.

"I think a lot of those people come in town and walk up and down because they're lonesome."

"This is too much for me," Ken said. He skipped over to the Indian Nut machine.

Dippy said, "If I was a pickpocket I'd work Market Street every day."

"You wouldn't find much," Ken said, distributing Indian Nuts among his friends.

"You're not kidding," George said.

Dippy flipped an Indian Nut nine feet in the air and caught it in his mouth.

"Let's go over to my house," Ken said. "Nobody's home. We'll listen to the radio."

The four of them started across the street.

Ralph stopped. He said, "I got a headache. I'm going home and go to bed."

He walked off.

Two blocks away from the candy store there was a park. It was a big park. It had a lake. The lake was a distorted circle, fringed with pavement. Placed along the pavement were benches. At times Ralph would walk to the park, dark in the thickness of late night. He would walk around the lake. He would light a cigarette. He would stand at the edge of the lake, looking at the smooth blackness sprinkled with glowing ribbons from lampposts. He would walk around the lake, moving slowly. He would walk around many times, and minutes would flick by and become an hour. The hour would double itself. He would be walking very slowly around the lake, alone.

He veered to the right and walked up to the park.

The grass and the leaves were thick black beneath the thick black sky.

He walked to the edge of the lake.

From his coat pocket he took his last cigarette, lighted it. He started to walk around the lake, very slowly.

He had fifteen cents in his pocket.

And he was telling himself not to go down there. What was he going to do after he got there? What was there, anyway? Why was it that he knew he should not go down there, and really did not want to go down there anyway, and yet had given up a pack of cigarettes so that he should have the carfare to go down there? Cigarettes were precious. He had given up a full pack. He was dragging at his final cigarette. And he had fifteen cents in his pocket. The carfare. It was not carfare yet. It would not be carfare until he slipped it through the arch in the cashier's booth and received his token and the turnstile turned to admit him to the subway. He could still walk back to the candy store and get a pack of cigarettes and go over to Ken's house. That was what he was going to do. He would walk once around the lake and then head back toward the corner.

Three times he walked around the lake and then he headed across the park, to the subway.

When he got off the train and walked up the steps to the street, he did not see many people, and he wondered what time it was. He asked a man, who pulled out a thick watch and told him it was a little past eleven. He stood still and told himself to go back into the subway and go home.

He walked along the dark street, away from the subway.

Then he was turning down a narrow street, moving slowly, counting the houses.

At the seventh house he stopped.

The front of the house was a door and a single window.

The window showed light coming from another room. That was all.

Ralph turned away, asking himself why he had come down here.

He was walking up the dark street. He heard a door open behind him. He heard footsteps, treading on three steps, then moving toward him. He turned around.

He saw her.

She was wearing a coat with the collar pulled up. The collar was torn, and so was the edge of a sleeve. He did not see the collar or the sleeve. He saw her face, her yellow eyes and her yellow hair.

And she moved toward him slowly, shaking her head slightly, and her eyes were sort of wide, and she was saying, "Don't I know – you?"

"Yes. We met last Saturday – at the party."

She nodded. "And you – went home."

"I guess I didn't feel well."

"What are you doing around here?" she said.

He looked at the ground. He looked up at her and he gulped hard and then he said, "I came to see you."

Her eyes were not wide now. But she was breathing hard, as if she had been running very fast. And she was saying, "I knew I was going to see you again."

"You did? You knew that?"

"Yes. I thought you might do something, like this."

"You mean you wanted me to?"

"Yes."

He looked at the pavement. He looked at the sky. He gulped hard again and then he said, "Where were you going – ?"

"I came out to take a walk. I was going to see Agnes."

"I'll walk you up to her house."

"No. I don't want to see her now."

"Because you're with me?"

"Yes."

They were walking slowly.

She said, "What do you do, Ralph?"

He looked at the ground. For a few moments he did not say anything. Then he muttered, "I don't do any – " He stopped there, looked up, and said, "I'm a songwriter."

"Oh – you are?"

"I write the words to songs. The lyrics."

"Gosh."

"I haven't been doing it for long."

"Oh, but it must be grand. Tell me about it, Ralph."

"Well, there's not much to it. Someone else makes up the tune and then I fit the words in. That's all."

"You've written a lot of songs?"

"No."

"But maybe I've heard some of those that you have written. Do they play your songs over the radio? Do they make records of them?"

"No."

"They print them, I guess? They give them to orchestras to play?"

"No."

"Well then – what do they do with them?"

"Nothing."

"Not a thing? You mean you write the songs and nothing is done with them? Why not?"

"Well, they're not good enough."

"Oh – "

"So I'm not really a songwriter. I don't make anything out of it."

"But you will someday. Your songs will get better and better and – " She looked up at him and said, "Isn't it grand to think about? Your songs getting better all the time and then they'll be played over the radio and the big

orchestras will make records out of them and everybody
will be listening."

"I hope so."

For a while they walked without saying anything.

Then Ralph said, "Wait here a minute."

He ran across the street, into a candy store. It had a
small, splintered glass soda fountain. An old man sat
behind the fountain, reading a newspaper. He looked up.

Ralph said, "Do me a favor."

"What."

"I got a token on me. It's all I got. I have a girl outside. I
want to get her a coke or something. The token's worth a
nickel, at least?"

"I guess so," the old man said. "Bring the girl in."

Ralph ran out of the store, crossed the street, to Edna.
He said, "I just went over there to see if that store had a
fountain. We'll get something."

"Oh, I don't – "

"Come on."

They crossed the street and entered the store. They sat
down at the fountain. Ralph said quickly, "How about a
coke?"

"That would be fine," she said.

Ralph looked at the old man. "A coke," he said.

The old man mixed two small cokes, pushed them
across the splintered glass.

Ralph started, "But I only said – "

The old man put his hand out. Ralph gave him the
token. The old man said, "Ten cents is – correct. Thank
you."

Ralph drank fast, finished his coke in a few gulps. Edna
sipped slowly, smiling at her glass.

"Good?" Ralph said.

She nodded. They left.

For a while they said nothing.

Then Edna said, "I haven't lived here long." She told him that the family had moved recently. And she told him why the family had moved, and of how her father was trying to get work in the auto-body plant. She was saying, "And I go in town every day to look for something. But – " she broke off and smiled at him and said, "you don't want to hear about that."

"Why not?"

"Because it's trouble. Trouble is something we shouldn't talk about. I guess we can't help ourselves if we think about it, but that doesn't say we have to talk about it."

"I guess not."

"You and I," she said. "We'll never talk about trouble."

"All right," he said.

They were walking up the street. They stood in front of her house.

She said, "When will I see you again?"

"Tomorrow night," he blurted. "We'll go someplace."

"No – we'll just – take a walk. I'll be too tired to go any place. I'll be walking around town all day."

"Then won't you be too tired to take a walk?"

"Well, I mean – "

"I know what you mean," he said, looking at the white step against the black pavement.

For a while they were quiet. Then she said, "Remember, Ralph, we said we weren't going to talk about trouble?"

"Yes."

"You'll come to see me tomorrow night, about nine, and we'll just take a walk?"

"All right."

"I guess I'll go in now. I guess you're tired."

"I'm not tired. Are you?"

"No," she said.

"But you gotta get up early tomorrow."

"Well, yes."

"It must be very late," he said.

"It doesn't seem like it."

"No."

"I'm not at all tired. I feel so good."

"So do I."

"Ralph, what are you going to do tomorrow?"

"See you."

"I mean in the day."

"Work on a song. Try to get an idea for words."

"Who writes the music?"

"Ken – you remember, the tall guy from last Saturday?"

"Oh yes. You work together."

"Yeah."

"You work hard, I guess."

"No."

"Why not?"

"I don't know."

"But, Ralph – "

He looked at her and turned his eyes away and looked at her and turned his eyes away and looked at her again and said, "I don't work hard because – well, I just don't like to work hard. I'm a bum."

"Oh, don't say that."

"Well, I will say it. I'm a bum."

"No you're not."

"I don't like to work. I'm a bum. I'm a no-good bum. I shouldn't have come here tonight. And I'm not coming tomorrow night. I'm not coming at all. What do I want to see you for? I won't be seeing you any more. Not at all."

Something bobbled in his throat and choked him. He turned fast and hurried away from the house. Several yards away he turned, and he saw her standing there in the doorway, looking at him. He started to walk back to her, and then he slowly turned again and walked away. He heard a door close. Once more he turned back, and walked to the house. The door was closed. All the lights were out.

He stood there, looking at the closed door, the blackness beyond the window.

Slowly, he walked up the street.

CHAPTER 9

At the piano Ken was playing his song. The door opened and Ralph walked in.

"I got the words finished."

"Let me see them," Ken said.

Ralph gave him the paper. He read it slowly. He put it on the piano, on the music-stand, played the song and sang the lyrics in a low, cracked voice.

"Well?" Ralph said.

Ken nodded. "They fit. They fit like a kid glove."

"Now what?"

"We get to work on another song."

"What are we gonna do with this one?"

"What can we do with it?" Ken said.

"Send it to a music company."

Ken said, "Don't make me laugh."

"What's the matter?"

"Please – don't make me laugh. We got a gorgeous ballad here, but a lot of good it's gonna do us to send it to those phonies in New York."

"What can we do with it?"

Ken said, "When I go down to Florida, I'll take it with me."

"When will that be?"

"Soon. Any day now."

"You've been going to Florida for a long time."

"Any day now."

Dippy and George walked in.

"God bless you, merry gentlemen," Dippy piped.

"Go to hell," Ken said.

George sat down and said, "Well, I'm out."

"What do you mean?" Ralph said.

"I'm out, that's all," George said. "I had a fight with the old man this morning and we started calling one another names and finally he told me I could get out. Before I knew what I was doing I went up and packed my things and now I'm over Dippy's."

"So tonight you'll go back home," Ken said.

"Yeah? You don't know my old man."

"You can come over our house," Ralph said.

"Nix," George said.

"I told him he can stay at my place," Dippy said.

"Yeah," Ken said. "That would make a big hit with your brother and your sister-in-law."

"Maybe I'll hit the road," George said.

Ken snapped his fingers and said, "It's a natural."

"What's a natural?" George said.

"My parents are going to Vineland to spend a few days with my sister and her husband. They have a farm there. A few days means a few weeks. Every time my old man gets on a farm he sleeps twenty-four hours a day. When he was a kid he worked on a farm and he had to get up at four in the morning and work until eight at night. So now he's getting even. He goes down to that farm in Vineland and he sleeps twenty-four hours a day."

"What's this got to do with me?" George said.

"You were born without brains," Ken said. "Don't you see? I'll be here by myself. So you'll move in. We'll have the house to ourselves."

"That sounds all right," George said.

"I think they're going tomorrow. Or they might leave this afternoon. I don't know. But anyway, we'll have this joint to ourselves. We'll throw a party every night."

"An excellent idea," Dippy said.

Ken said, "I don't know how we're gonna eat. My old man won't leave me a dime. But we'll manage some way. And as long as they don't cut off the electricity, and leave a little coal in the cellar, we'll do all right."

"Do you think your parents will leave tonight?" George said.

"Maybe."

Dippy said, "We'll have a party every night, with pretty girls."

George and Ken laughed.

Ken said, "You know, with an empty house like this, we can work a few angles."

"Whaddya mean?" George said.

"Well, we can have some of the boys in here for crap games, and we can cut the games. We can make about ten bucks a night that way. Or then we could have them playing blackjack or poker in the other room, and we could cut on that. Say, you know what we could do? We could have a game in every room in the house. Figure it out. If we cut on every game we could clean up. For Christ's sake, figure how many rooms there are in this house. Three downstairs, three upstairs, including the bathroom. That's six rooms. A game in every room, and we'll cut about ten bucks a game. That's sixty bucks a night. Seven nights a week makes four hundred and twenty clams. Do you get that? Four hundred and twenty pieces of clam. And that's figuring conservative."

"You think it can be worked?" George said.

"Do I think it can be worked? Don't be a fool. This is the real velvet. All we do is spread the word around, at the poolroom, on the corner, up at the diner and the cigar store on Broad Street and we'll have them flocking here like sparrows. Ten bucks a room, six rooms –"

"And what about the cellar?" George said.

"The cellar – the cellar – " Ken muttered. "Sure, the

cellar." He snapped his fingers. "Here's what we do. We throw three games into the cellar. That gives us three bedrooms empty. But they won't be empty for long."

"What's the pitch?" George said.

"Use your head," Ken said, snapping his fingers again. "This whole thing is a natural. We'll go downtown and pick up three hookers and bring them up here and put them in the bedrooms. And we'll split the take."

"What are you gonna do?" George shouted, getting excited. "Are you gonna make a joint out of this place?"

"Listen to this guy," Ken yelled. "He's got a chance to make a snappy two hundred clams – "

"You're crazy," George said. "We'll have the cops in here and we'll all get locked up, so help me."

For a while there was quiet.

Then George said, "You better give up the idea."

Ken looked across the room, at the piano. He said, "A guy's gotta do something. He's gotta take his risks. He's gotta do something." He shook his head. In a very low voice he said, "Take a chance."

Again there was quiet for a while.

In the next room Dippy was on the phone. He was saying, "Indeed?"

George and Ken laughed. They went into the next room to listen to Dippy.

In the living room Ralph sat alone and looked out the window, at the gray pavement and the dull black street and the gray sky. He was thinking of when he was sixteen years old and had joined the mineralogy club in high school. He had become very interested in mineralogy. He went down to the Academy of Natural Sciences and read all about the stones. He used to visit a lapidary and ask to see uncut stones. One day the old man there told him where he could find amethyst. The old man claimed that along the banks of the Wissahickon there was amethyst.

Ralph took a trolley and hiked along the Wissahickon. It was winter. The Wissahickon Creek was half-frozen. Ralph walked along the bank of the creek. He was alone. Out here everything was dry and cold and clean. He forgot about the amethyst. He just wanted to walk along by the bank of the creek. Dead leaves swayed in praying mobs around the trunks of bare trees. Everything was still and quiet, except for the clear icy water splashing over the rocks and pebbles in the creek. He walked on, looking at the water, and the trees, and the rocks, and the quiet loveliness of the Wissahickon Creek and its valley, and he wanted to stay here. He wanted to build a cave, beneath one of the big rocks, and there he would stay, all alone, yet not alone, for he would have the crinkling song of the creek, and the defiant song of birds almost frozen yet reluctant to leave the creek and the valley. In his cave in the valley by the creek he would stay always, all alone, yet not alone, and he would have all he wanted.

Remembering that, he longed again for the creek and the valley. He stood up, moved past the window, to the door. He would go again to the Wissahickon.

From the next room Ken said, "Where you going?"

"Nowhere special."

Into the phone Dippy said, "You mean to say that you don't know what a system engineer is?"

George and Ken were laughing. Ken said, "Listen to this, Ralph. This is good."

Ralph had his hand on the doorknob. He started to turn it and then his fingers fell away and he walked toward George and Ken and Dippy.

George said, "Get the details."

Into the phone Dippy said, "How old are you and how tall and how much do you weigh?"

He cupped his hand over the mouthpiece and turned to

his friends and said, "This is something out of the ordinary."

"Fix it up," Ken said.

"Saturday night – up here. That's tomorrow night, ain't it?" George said.

"We'll have the house to ourselves," Ken said.

Ralph murmured, "Count me out."

"We'll have them here all night," George said, while Dippy continued his negotiations over the phone.

"I'm not in on it," Ralph said.

"Say, what's wrong with you?" Ken said.

"Nothing."

"Don't hand me that."

"I tell you nothing's wrong," Ralph said.

"What are you sore about?"

"Who said I was sore?"

"Well then, what's the matter?"

"Nothing."

"I know what it is," Ken said. "It's the song we wrote. You're sore because I'm not sending the song to a music company."

"I'm not sore, about the song," Ralph said. "I'm not sore about anything."

George said, "He's snakebitten."

"That's it," Ken said. "That's it. You're snakebitten about something. What is it?"

"Nothing," Ralph said. He turned away and walked to the front door.

"Hey, wait a minute," Ken called. "Where you going?"

Ralph opened the door and went out.

In his room Ralph bit at a pencil and looked at the blank paper. He was telling himself that if he could fit words to a tune, then maybe Ken could fit a tune to these words. As yet there were no words on the paper. But there soon would be. He knew what he wanted to put down on the paper. The words were rolling around in his mind. He had to put them down on the paper. They would flow from his mind to his arm to his hand to the pencil onto the paper. He would take the words over to Ken who would develop a tune. He was putting the words down now. This was all he wanted to do. He wanted to be here alone in his room, putting the things that were in his mind into words that would crawl from the pencil onto the paper. He crossed out some words and then he looked out the window, at the grey sky. And he looked back at the paper, then back at the sky again and saw that the grey was getting deeper. He looked at the words on the paper and he took the paper in his hand and slowly crumpled it up and then tore it in little pieces. He opened the window and threw the pieces of paper out and watched them sail down to the alley, a wide-spread fleet.

He walked out of the room.

At nine o'clock Edna looked out the window and saw the dark, narrow, empty street. Turning quickly away from the window, she told herself that she was foolish. She sighed and tried to tell herself that one always sighed when one was so very tired. She had walked a lot today. Up and down the downtown streets. In and out of one place after another. Not a chance. Nothing. Not even a promise of something in the future. Everything was taken. There were so many girls who were out after jobs. Maybe there would be something tomorrow. There had to be something. She had to find something. Her father had not yet landed a job. The money was going to run out soon and she had to find something, anything, just so it was something. She sighed again. The soles of her feet were burning and she thought of all the walking that she would do tomorrow, and the soles of her feet burned more. She looked out the window again and then glanced at the battered alarm clock that rested on a chair. It was twenty minutes past nine.

He was not coming here tonight. He was not coming here at all. She would never see him again.

She stood up. The house was cold. But even so it felt warm and sticky and close in here. She wondered why that was. She wondered why she wanted to go outside. She went into the next room and put on her torn coat and then went out. And as she was walking down the steps she saw him.

Leaning against the wall, a few houses away, looking at the ground.

She walked toward him.

He looked up and he was startled, and there was fright in his eyes, and he started to turn away.

"Oh, Ralph, please don't go."

"I –"

"Why are you standing out here, like this?"

"I don't know."

"You don't even have an overcoat on. Aren't you cold?"

"No."

"You're cold, Ralph. I can see. Come in my house."

"No – I'll be going."

"Please don't, Ralph. You came down here to see me, didn't you?"

"Yes."

"And you were here at nine o'clock, just like you said you'd be, even though you said later that –"

"Well, I –"

"You were here at nine, weren't you? Since nine you were standing out here like this, waiting."

"I'm going home now."

"Please don't, Ralph. Please come in my house."

"I don't want to."

"Yes you do. I know you do. And it's warm in there. Well anyway, it's warmer than it is out here. Why haven't you got your overcoat on? You had one on last night. Did you lose it?"

"No. I forgot it."

She pushed him toward the house. On the steps he stopped. Then she opened the door and pushed him into the house. She closed the door fast.

"Now," she said.

He looked at the floor. He looked at her eyes and then he looked at the floor again and he said, "You waited for me."

"Yes."

"You knew I was going to be here."

"Come in the kitchen. You're cold. I'll make tea."

"Oh, no."

"I want some for myself anyway. If you don't want any you can watch me."

He followed her into the kitchen.

She made tea. As the water boiled she said, "Do you like it without lemon or without cream?"

"Without lemon," he said.

They smiled at each other.

They sat at the small table, sipping tea.

"You needed this," she said. "You're not cold now, are you?"

"No."

"Ralph, if I hadn't come outside, were you going to walk away?"

"I think so, yes."

"Why?"

"I don't know."

"You do. Tell me."

"I was afraid."

"Afraid of what? Not afraid of me?"

"Not exactly."

"Then what?"

"I don't know, Edna. I just don't know."

"Ralph – "

They were looking at each other, forgetting the tea.

"Did you know I was outside?" he said.

"No – I – I don't think so – no, of course, I didn't know you were outside."

"Well then, what made you come out?"

"I just wanted to – I don't know, Ralph. I just sort of put on my coat. Felt like going outside, or – no, I didn't really. I don't know. I went outside, and I don't know why. I didn't know you were out there, and I don't know why I went out."

"I can't understand it," he said.

"Neither can I."

"Maybe that's what I'm afraid of."

"What, Ralph?"

"Well, me, standing there, wanting to go away. I didn't even want to come down here in the first place. I went out of the house – I don't even remember where I went. But I started to walk. I just kept on walking. I didn't know I was coming here. I didn't know that I forgot to take my overcoat. I was on this street – "

"You walked all the way?"

"I didn't fly."

"And you walked the entire distance."

"When I saw your house, I realized where I was. I wanted to go away."

"Why are you so afraid?"

"Edna – I don't know."

"You do know. You won't tell me."

He was looking at her and looking away and looking at her again. He stood up. He looked at the floor. He looked around the room, wildly, as if he was searching for a channel of flight.

"I gotta be going," he said.

He walked out of the room, and through the small house, and he was almost running as he neared the front door. And she was running after him, and he stopped, and turned around.

She said, "Please don't go away from me."

He looked at her and looked at the floor and looked at her again. "Take care of yourself," he said. It sounded odd to him.

The front door was open and he was walking down the steps. Edna stood in the doorway. She said, "I hope someday you'll come back."

CHAPTER 10

George carried a battered suitcase into Ken's house.

Ken laughed.

"What's so funny?" George said.

"You look like one of these guys that just got off Ellis Island."

"That's just the way I feel," George said. "Is the coast clear?"

"Clear as glass," Ken said. "My parents left for Vineland less than an hour ago. And they'll stay three weeks if they stay a day."

"Did they leave you anything?"

"Yeah, the house."

"I mean something in the icebox, or a few bucks."

"Of course not. Don't be a fool."

George scratched his head. "How are we gonna live?"

Ken glared at him disgustedly. "We're gonna take berries off the trees," he said. He bit open a pack of cigarettes, and he and George lit up. "Dippy's smuggling some food out of his house and he's bringing it over here. At least we'll eat tonight. Tomorrow I'm calling up my sister in West Philly and tell her to come across with a fin unless she wants her brother to starve to death. Look, I want to show you something."

He took George into the next room, and he opened up the bottom drawer of the china closet. In the drawer were three bottles of Irish whiskey and a bottle of gin.

"That looks good," George said.

"My old man slipped up. Usually he watches that stuff

like a hawk. But this time he forgot to take it along with him. Next time he'll know better." Ken laughed.

"You're not gonna open the bottles, are you?"

"Now what do you think?" Ken said. "We got a big party here tonight, son. We're gonna have a bar and all, and if we need more liquor, we'll send the servants out – "

"Sure," George said.

They laughed.

Ken sat down at the piano and started to play his new tune. He reached on top the piano and took the paper on which were written the lyrics. He started to sing.

"That's not bad," George said.

"I never knew Ralph could do stuff like this," Ken said.

He banged hard on the piano and sang in a cracked voice.

Dippy walked in. He said, "Good morning, men." He carried a paper bag. George and Ken leaped at the bag. There were four slices of white bread. There were three cans of peaches.

Ken looked at the labels on the cans. "Peaches," he said. "Now what the hell are we gonna do with peaches?"

"Eat them," Dippy said.

"Four pieces of bread and three cans of peaches." Ken glared at the label on the can.

"You can make peach sandwiches," Dippy said.

George laughed.

"Peaches and bread." Ken mumbled.

"Not necessarily," Dippy said.

"All right, brains. Let's hear a wise remark now," Ken snapped.

Dippy said, "We'll go up to Broad Street. My mother buys her stuff at the big market up there. I'll take the peaches in and say that I bought four cans yesterday and that I opened one can and found a lot of worms in there.

I'll become indignant. I'll ask for something else in return for the peaches."

"Sometimes this guy's a wizard," George said.

They went up to Broad Street and Dippy made his protest. In exchange for the peaches he received two cans of soup and a loaf of bread. The three of them hurried back to Ken's house and feasted. When they were puffed with the soup and the bread, Ken showed Dippy the liquor.

"Now we'll have cocktails," Dippy said.

"You fool you. They don't drink cocktails after they eat. They drink them before," Ken said.

"What's the difference?" Dippy said.

Ken opened the bottle of gin. He said, "Straight gin is the correct thing to drink after eating. Anybody who knows anything about it will tell you that. You gotta know how to live."

He poured three glasses of gin.

"This tastes like perfume," Dippy said.

"You're not kidding," George said.

Ken glared at them. "A lot you guys know about it," he said. "The whole trouble is, you don't know how to drink. You're not drinking men."

"I know how to drink," Dippy said. "I put it in my mouth and let it go down my throat. That's all there is to it."

"That's how much you know," Ken said.

"You tell us about it," George said.

They were in the living room, smoking cigarettes. George turned on the radio. Jazz pumped out.

"Where's Ralph?" George said.

Ken shrugged. "I don't know."

"Is he coming tonight?" Dippy said.

"No," Ken said. "Something's the matter with that guy. He's snakebitten."

"What is this?" Dippy said.

George muttered, "One thing I know. If somebody walked up to me and threw a couple hundred bucks in my lap, I'd be very much obliged."

Ken sighed. "Florida's the place. Florida's the only place."

"When are we going?" Dippy said.

"Any day now," Ken said.

They sat there, looking at the slow-moving curtain of grey smoke, looking at it as it drifted toward the ceiling and faded away. They lifted the gin glasses and grinned at each other.

Ralph was in his room, putting words on paper. He had taken three pieces of paper from Addie's loose-leaf notebook. The three pieces of paper were filled, front and back. Ralph looked at the words he had put down. He shook his head slowly. He tore up the three pieces of paper. He walked out of his room. The house was quiet. His father and mother were asleep. Addie was at a rollerskating rink. Evvie was on a date. The hall light was dim orange. He walked through the hall and down the steps. He put on his overcoat and went out. It was very cold. He walked to the corner. It was empty. He remembered about the party. He started toward Ken's house. He wished he had a cigarette. In the park there was nothing to break the biting wind, and it whizzed hard at him. He turned up the collar of his coat, walked to the lake. The lake was freezing. The blackness of the ice and the grass and leaves and sky was hard and cold. He walked around the lake, watching his shoes glimmering against the cement. He looked up. There was nobody around. The lake and the park were empty of people and the sky was empty of stars. The cold sliced through him and he figured he would walk once more around the lake and then go home and go to sleep. Then he swerved off and moved slowly across the park and two blocks down to the corner. He glanced into the candy store, at the clock on the wall, and saw that it was eleven-thirty. He leaned against the wall and shivered and put his hands in his pockets.

He saw Dippy and George and Ken as they approached the corner. They were singing and shouting and cursing. They were staggering. Dippy cupped his hands to his mouth and shouted, "Extra! Extra! Big earthquake!"

Windows and doors were opening. People were sticking their heads out.

"Paper – paper," a man said. "Hurry up with that paper."

"Go to hell," Dippy said.

George and Ken were howling, throwing their heads back and laughing with all their might.

The three of them weaved over to Ralph.

He looked them up and down and said, "You guys are a mess."

"How dare you say a thing like that?" Dippy said.

Ralph laughed. "What happened?" he said. "Where's the party?"

Ken said, "The bitches didn't show up. We got the address of one of them, though. We're going down there and set her house on fire."

"That would be nice," Ralph said. "So they stood you up." He laughed.

"Yep, the girls stood us up," George sang, "but the liquor came through, didn't it, boys?"

"I most certainly agree with you," Dippy said.

"And we got more," Ken yelled.

"We got gallons," George said.

"Hundreds of gallons," Dippy said.

"Really?" Ralph said.

"Sure," Ken shouted. "Let's show him! Onward!"

They pulled Ralph along. Dippy ran in front and waved an imaginary sword. "Onward!" he yelled.

They went charging into Ken's house.

There was still a lot of liquor left. They started to drink. Ken grabbed a bottle of Irish and pushed it toward Ralph.

"Nix," Ralph said.

"Don't be a fool," Ken said.

Ralph looked at the bottle. He didn't want to drink. Every time he started with liquor he wound up very sick. When he started he couldn't stop. It had not happened many times, but when it did happen it was bad. He remembered one time at a party he had started in and afterward they told him he had killed off more than a quart. He knew he had no right to monkey around with the stuff. He had his teeth on the lip of the bottle, and he threw his head back. The liquor flowed into his mouth, flaming down his throat. He gulped it fast, kept gulping.

"Look at this guy go," Ken said.

Ralph had the glass between his teeth and out of the bottle came the Irish whiskey, flowing fast down his throat.

Trying to stand on his head, in the center of the room. George fell on his face.

Dippy was making a speech.

Ken was watching Ralph gulp liquor.

George was sliding into third.

Dippy silenced a heckler.

Ken put his hand to the side of his face. His eyes, focused on the liquor draining from the bottle tilted to Ralph's head, were steadily widening.

George played it deep. It was a hard ground ball, searing close to third. It took a bad hop and George played it brilliantly. He addressed himself to the ball, got his glove under it, had it in his right hand. He pegged it to first. Shibe Park rocked with acclaim. George bowed and fell on his face.

Dippy waved his arms and urged his listeners to try a new cereal.

Ken turned away, slowly shaking his head.

The bottle, tilted almost vertically, was half-empty. Ralph took it away from his teeth. He looked at Dippy. He looked at the bottle again. He saw George face down on the floor. He saw Ken trying to find a dial on the radio. He saw the ceiling and the walls and the floor and the bottle again. He lifted it to his mouth, and the glass lip was between his teeth. The liquor blazed down his throat.

George and Ken were asleep. They were on the floor. Ken's shoe was on George's chin. They slept soundly.

Dippy sat with his ear close to the radio loudspeaker. Police calls were coming through. Dippy made out he was a policeman, racing to the scene of disturbance.

Upstairs there was a thud.

Dippy hurried upstairs. Ralph was on the bathroom floor, cursing. He was underneath the washbowl. He lifted his head and bumped it against the washbowl. He moaned and went flat on the floor. He was out. Dippy stood there, looking at him. Then Dippy let cold water run into the washbowl. He lifted Ralph and pushed his head into the cold water. There was only a slight bump on Ralph's head. The liquor, more than the collision, had knocked him out. His eyes were open now and he was mumbling. Water dripped from his head.

He shook his head and blinked a few times and said, "I'm all right now."

"More or less," Dippy said.

Ralph walked out of the bathroom and into the hall and fell to his knees. He got up and took a few more steps and fell flat.

"I'm all right," he said. Dippy nodded.

"Everybody's all right," Ralph said.

"Everybody."

"Everybody in the whole world," Ralph said.

"Why not?" Dippy said.

Ralph straightened and was on his feet and weaving toward the stairs. He jolted forward and started to fall down the stairs and Dippy caught him. Dippy helped him down the stairs. In the living room Ralph pushed Dippy away and said, "I'm all right."

"Of course," Dippy said.

"What time is it?" Ralph said.

Dippy skipped into the kitchen and skipped out again and sang, "It's three o'clock in the morning."

"Late," Ralph said.

"Somewhat," Dippy said.

Ralph moved toward the front door. He fell. He got up again. He fell again. He got up again. He sat down and his legs were sprawled out and he said, "It's no use, pardner. I'm done. Go on alone. There must be water ahead."

Dippy lifted Ralph from the floor. He put his arm around Ralph and held him up. Together they staggered out of the house. They staggered down the steps and down the dark street. Ralph fell. Dippy fell on top. They got up.

"Onward," Dippy said.

When they were near Dippy's house, Ralph collapsed again. Dippy dragged him into the house, lifted him to the sofa. Dippy rested at the foot of the sofa, flat on his back. He closed his eyes and within a minute he was fast asleep.

At almost four in the morning, Lenore walked down the street, toward the house. She walked slowly. She was all in. She was ready to drop. She had been with the Italian since ten. The Italian lived a block away. He was thirty-three years old. He was married but he didn't live with his wife. He was six feet tall and he weighed more than 200 pounds and he was like rock. His hair and eyes were very black and gleaming, and his chin and cheeks were blue-white with heavy beard that was shaven twice each day.

The Italian was a construction foreman. He was rough. Lenore liked him. She liked his hands. Sometimes he got a bit too rough, but Lenore knew how to manage that. She knew how to manage him and all the rest of them. She had something on each and every one of them. All they had to do was open their mouths just once and she would give them away. They all knew that. Lenore always made sure she had something on a man before she added him to her list. The Italian, for instance. The Italian wanted to get his wife back. His wife was a pretty little Italian girl who lived with the two kids and the grandmother in South Philly. Lenore knew the address. She told the Italian if he ever tried to pull any monkey business, she would go down to South Philly and open her mouth. The Italian would never get his wife back. Whenever Lenore yelled this at him, the big, rock-like Italian would start to cry. Lenore would laugh at him. She laughed at all of them. Most of all she laughed at Clarence.

She kept telling Clarence that she would treat him better on condition that he move with her into a smart apartment. Then she would really treat him better. He cursed and yelled and lately he was getting fits of screaming. He would start to scream and punch his fists together and Lenore would sit there and laugh at him. Lenore kept telling him what a fool he was. And she would be standing in front of the mirror with very little on. Pretending that she did not know he was watching, she would be putting her hands on herself. She was fat, but her build was interesting. It would go on like this until he couldn't stand it any longer and he would go downstairs and try to sleep on the sofa. She would be laughing and telling herself it wouldn't be long now until he went with her to look for a smart apartment, with yellow wallpaper and a yellow piano. It wouldn't be long now. Tonight he was waiting up for her. As always, when she went to spend an evening with the Italian or with one of the others, she had told Clarence she was going to visit her sick sister. The sick sister situation was perfect. The sister was actually very sick. She was allowed to see nobody but Lenore. And sometimes she was so sick that Lenore would have to stay there all night with her, afraid to leave her alone.

Played out, looking forward to a soft bed and sleeping all day tomorrow, Lenore walked into the house.

She looked at Dippy, flat on his back, on the floor. She heard a moan from the sofa.

She looked at the other one on the sofa. She put her hands on her hips and stood there looking at him.

"What are you looking at?" Dippy said.

Lenore stepped away from the sofa. Dippy was still flat on his back but his eyes were open. She stared at him. Then she said, "What's bothering you?"

"Not a thing," Dippy said. "How do you feel?"

"I feel fine."

"That's too bad," Dippy said.

"Die."

"After you."

"Who's that drunken bum on the couch?"

"Ralph. You know him."

She stood there, looking at Ralph. She said, "Drunken bum."

"Don't wake him up," Dippy said.

She looked at Dippy. She said, "What the hell do I want to wake him up for?"

"I don't know."

Lenore said, "What's the big idea bringing him here? Whaddya think this is, anyway?"

"A house."

"That don't say you can bring him in here and let him mess up the whole goddam place."

"Go away and don't annoy me."

"I'll go away and won't annoy you – I'll kick you right in your face, you slimy worm. You got one lousy hell of a nerve, you have, bringing in drunken bums and putting them all over the house – "

"I got about thirty of them in the kitchen," Dippy said.

"I got a good mind to kick this bum right out into the gutter, where he belongs."

"Good night," Dippy said.

"I'm not ready to go up yet," Lenore yapped. "I got a few things to say to you."

"Well, say them fast. My time is limited."

"I'll give you your time. One of these days I'll give you a crack across that fresh mouth of yours."

"That would be unfortunate."

"I'm getting good and fed up with you," Lenore said. "I'm getting fed up with a lot of things around here. And if you think I'll keep on putting up with it, you got another think coming. I don't have to stand for this sort of thing. I don't have to stand for anything from you. And from your mother too. Clarence pays the rent in this house. I'm his wife. We're giving you a break, you and your mother. We're letting you stay here with us. We don't have to."

"Do me a big favor," Dippy said. "Walk up to the top of the steps and fall down."

"Why, you rat bastard!"

"Make sure it's from the top," Dippy said. He was resting comfortably on his back, with his hands under his head and his feet propped up.

Lenore stood over him. Her hands were on her hips.

"You'd like that. You'd like to see me fall down a flight of steps. You'd get a kick out of that, wouldn't you?"

"I imagine so," Dippy said.

Lenore shouted, "Well, get a kick out of this!" Her foot swished out fast.

Waiting for it, Dippy was ready. He rolled to the side, at the same time reaching out and grabbing her ankle as she kicked at him. He pulled hard. Lenore lost her balance and sat down with a loud bump. She screeched and made a lunge for Dippy, and he rolled away and she tripped and fell again. She got up fast, cursing and screaming, and ran after him. He scooted into the next room and ran around the table. Upstairs the mother and Clarence were yelling, wanting to know what all the noise was about. Unsmilingly, Dippy thumbed his nose at Lenore. He foxed his way into the living room and pulled the front door open and raced out.

Lenore was all in. She cursed and sobbed and fell to the floor.

On the sofa, Ralph slowly sat up.

Mascara mixed with tears of rage rolled down Lenore's face. The peroxide blonde hair fell over her eyes.

She looked at Ralph. She said, "Don't sit there. Help me up."

He went over to her and started to help her up. He had her by the wrists. She pulled away. Then she grabbed at his elbows, and pushed his arms toward her, she forced him to place his hands under her armpits. As she slowly stood up, she pushed herself against him, and then she had her arms around his middle and she was rubbing herself against him. Her belly moved in circles, came against him and pumped away, and came against him.

Still sort of sick, and very dizzy, he didn't catch on. He thought she was holding tight to keep him from falling. He didn't need any help. He wanted to go back to sleep. He squirmed away from her. He took hold of her wrists and forced her arms away and stepped back.

Lenore looked him up and down. Her face twisted, and her thick-lipsticked lips spread out and then rolled together and she put her hands on her hips and said, "Why you dirty drunken bum – "

He swayed. He had a headache. He was blinking. Lenore patterned her mouth into an odd smile and pushed her hands against his chest, hard.

He fell back, crashed against a radiator, and rocked back and forth. He was not blinking now. His eyes were wide. Lenore looked at his eyes and she started to move away. His shoulders were hunched, and he took a step toward her. She moved back, faster. He closed his eyes, opened them again and saw her and closed them again so that he should not see her. He was shivering now, and his eyes were shut tight. He was shaking his head, telling himself to get out of here fast.

Lenore watched him hurry out of the house. She walked to the door and watched him moving down the street. Lenore smiled. As she re-entered the house, her smile widened, and then it faded, and her lips were set contentedly.

CHAPTER 11

Late Sunday afternoon, Dippy walked into Ken's house and a few minutes later Ralph came in.

Ken was at the piano, playing the song, singing the words that Ralph had submitted to him.

George was on the sofa. There was a wet towel around his head.

"Jesus Christ Almighty," he said.

Ken looked at Ralph. He said, "You know how much you had last night?"

"I don't know," Ralph said.

"I bet you had a quart, easy."

"I think I'm dying," George said.

"I'm sorry to hear that," Dippy said.

Ken looked closely at Ralph and said, "How do you feel?"

"I feel all right."

George said, "Oh, God –"

"What is this?" Dippy said.

Ralph leaned against the window sill and said, "Starting tomorrow, they're taking guys on down at Blayner's. My sister told me. She got the wire from a girl friend of hers who works there. If we all go down early tomorrow morning we might get something."

George sat up. "No kidding," he said.

Ken said, "Look at him. He's all excited."

"It's a job," George said.

"You wanna come down with me tomorrow?" Ralph said.

"I'm in," George said.

"Saps," Ken said. "They'll go down to Blayner's and wait in line all day. If they're real lucky they'll get jobs for the Christmas rush. Two weeks' work. A big deal. Twelve and a half bucks a week. Working their heads off in the shipping room."

"It's twenty-five bucks," George said.

Ralph said, "You worked there last year, Ken. It wasn't so bad, was it?"

"It was miserable," Ken said.

"Yeah, I know," Ralph said, putting his hands in his pockets and slouching against the window sill. "But even so, it's something."

"Sure," George said, "it's something."

"It's nothing," Ken said. "It's worse than nothing. I can see you guys, getting up at six-thirty in the morning and I mean a cold morning – "

"Aw shut up," George said.

" – a real cold morning," Ken said. "Getting up and going down to that madhouse and working like dogs. And at the end of the week you get twelve and a half bucks. Right away we slice six bits off that for carfare. And what about lunch? You put in a morning's work at Blayner's, you can eat a horse."

"Well, we'll take lunch from home," George said.

Ralph said, "I'll split my lunch with you, George."

"No, I won't let you do that," George said.

"Look at these two guys," Ken said. "They look starved already."

"George, don't you worry about lunch," Ralph said.

"All right, you guys," Ken said. "Don't listen to me. Go down to Blayner's. Wait in line. Get the hunger jobs. And when the two weeks are up, you'll go to the poolroom. Remember last year? Remember how we went up the poolroom? We had about thirty-five clams between the three of us. Two weeks of slavery. Thirty-five clams. We thought we could run it up. We walked out of the poolroom without a goddam cent."

Ralph said, "Maybe this year we can talk ourselves into steady jobs."

"Yeah, you got a good case." Ken waved in disgust.

George yelled, "Well for Christ's sake, we gotta do something! We gotta get some kind of action! Something's gotta happen!"

"Listen to this guy," Ken said. "Listen to this jerk. He's all worked up. I'll tell you what will happen. Nothing. Absolutely nothing. In two weeks you'll be back on the corner, eating Indian Nuts without a red cent in your pocket. There's only one way that things happen. That's when you make them happen."

"Here it comes again," George said.

"I'm trying to show you guys what's uptown. I'm telling you that the only move is to slide out of this hungry set-up and shoot down to Florida."

"Florida," Dippy said, "Florida, with the beach."

"Yeah, Florida," Ken said. "That's the place where I'm headed."

"I'm going with you," Dippy said.

"When are you going?" Ralph said.

Ken stood up. He raised the cigarette butt high in the air and his long arm swished down and he slammed the butt to the floor and stamped hard on it and said, "Goddammit, I'm going tomorrow!"

"I'm going with you," Dippy said.

From all parts of the city, from the suburbs and the small towns across the river and to the south of the city, from all parts, the smoky factory sections, the close-packed neighborhoods, from all over the city the people poured into the center of town and huddled against each other in the slicing cold. There was tinsel and colored paper and bright lights in the windows of the stores along Market Street. All along the street there were rows of colored lights on ropes attached to telegraph poles. From the amplifiers came Christmas carols and jingling bells and the voice of Santa Claus. In the cold the people poured along the street, close against each other. They were smiling or trying hard to smile. They were happy or trying hard to be happy. Above them the lights glittered. The carols leaped merrily. Many people joined in the singing. On the corners the Santa Clauses hopped up and down from cold. They blew on their hands and smiled at the children.

In the stores the salesgirls sweated.

The shipping clerks bent and ran and reached and grabbed and ripped and tore and tied and cursed and reached and grabbed and tied and threw and cursed and tied and reached and grabbed and threw and cursed.

From the amplifiers the ribbon of sound narrowed as it twisted its way down into the stock rooms of the big stores. Santa Claus was asking a little boy if he had been a good little boy to his father.

Ralph grabbed at a package and threw it into the arms of a big Polish fellow named Paul who had blue eyes and freckles.

Santa Claus said, "And have you been good to your little sister?"

Paul said, "If I was that kid I'd clip Santa Claus in the teeth."

Ralph wound hemp around a big package.

In the stock room the men heaved and sweated and grabbed and threw and heaved.

Ralph grabbed at a package.

Paul said, "This your first day?"

"Yeah."

"You worked here before?"

"Last Christmas," Ralph said. "A little in between. Easter too."

"I work here all the time," Paul said.

"How do you like it?"

"It's wonderful," Paul said. He wiped sweat from his face.

Ralph heaved at a big package and said, "Some of these are sort of heavy."

"That ain't nothing," Paul said. "Wait'll they start giving us the hurry-up talk."

"Last Christmas there were more guys here," Ralph said.

Paul nodded. "Yup, that's just it. Last Christmas they had more guys. This year the cheap sons of bitches figure they'll save themselves some dough. They hire less guys and give us the hurry-up talk. Last week there was a guy here named Sol, strong like an ox. He just got the job. He was scared. He was out of work for a long time and he had a wife and two kids and he wanted to make good. He wanted to keep the job. I told him to slow down or he'd wear himself out. He didn't even hear me talking to him. So then it's a busy day and one of them big shots from upstairs comes down and tells us to get a move on. Just when that happened this Sol was coasting. He was all in and he was taking a minute or so time out. This guy from upstairs points at Sol and tells him to get a move on. You shoulda seen that Sol jump. He starts working a mile a minute. He grabs at big packages like they were feathers. Sol grabs at a package that needs three guys instead of one. What happens? He drops to the floor like an earthquake hit him. It's a rupture. So now he's up the creek."

Ralph pulled twine. "After Christmas it ain't so busy."

"Don't worry. You won't be here after Christmas," Paul said.

"I guess not."

"And you're better off," Paul said. "This ain't no job for a human. They oughta train gorillas for this sorta work."

Ralph laughed.

"It ain't no joke. You work down here for three years, like I been doing, and you'll see it ain't no joke. The same thing all the time, day in and day out, with these bastards from upstairs coming down to tell us how slow we are. There's a special one I got it in for. He comes down here and starts calling us a lot of names. He thinks he's tough. He's a sort of bulky guy, about thirty, and I heard he used to fight in the amateurs. I don't know how he got the job upstairs. He don't have any brains. All he knows is to come down here and get tough with us. All the guys are scared of him. I'm not. I don't have to take his guff. One of these days he's gonna get my goat once too often. Then you'll see what'll happen. You married?"

"No."

"You're lucky. I'm hitched. If I only had myself to worry about I'd quit right now. I'm only thirty-one. You know what I'd do? I'd hop a freight. I'd get down to Texas. I'd hitch onto a tanker down in the Gulf. Then I'd shove. That's what I wanna do. But I hadda go get married and now she's gonna have a kid." He tugged viciously at a big package.

Santa Claus said, "And what would you like, young man?"

"Aw, shove it," Paul said.

Ralph's mother had packed a big lunch. She wondered why he asked for so much food. She did not know that he shared his lunch with George. When he got home at night he did not eat much. Mrs Creel thought it was because of the big lunch. She did not know that he was too tired to eat.

For a while he would sit around and read the newspaper and listen to the radio. Then he would walk over to Ken's house. He would stay there for an hour or so. Then he would walk out to the park. He would walk around the lake. He would walk around a few times and then without knowing it he would be walking away from the lake and the park and in the opposite direction from the corner, aiming toward a dark narrow street where the houses were a solid, unbroken wall of dark grey brick with doors and windows. He would walk in this direction for a block or two and then he would stop and turn around and head back toward the park and the lake.

Very tired, he would look forward to sleep.

With each day there was more work. In the stock room the men heaved and sweated and cursed and heaved. The packages flowed in and out and in and out. From outside came the drone of the pouring crowd and the amplified carol-singing and jingling bells and the voice of Santa Claus. The men in the stock room heaved and pushed and sweated. The packages whizzed through. Santa Claus asked the children what they wanted for Christmas. The packages tumbled and rocked and jolted and rolled through the curse-filled and sweat-filled rooms of stock and shipping. Outside, the crowd poured along the seething street.

"Well, sonny," Santa Claus said, "what am I going to give you?"

"Nothing. Absolutely nothing," Paul said. "Listen to that phony."

Ralph twisted a package around and pushed it toward Paul. He said, "Coming through fast now."

"Sure," Paul said.

Footsteps clattered down the stairs. Someone whispered, "It's Fred —"

Fred ran down the stairs. Halfway down he stopped

and addressed himself to the men. "You lazy sons of bitches," he said.

"That's the guy," Paul mumbled, nudging Ralph. "That's the guy I got it in for."

"Come on, you bums," Fred said, walking slowly down the stairs. "Whaddya think this is? We're already behind on these rush send-outs. The trucks are waitin' and you're takin' your goddam time. Let's see some action!"

He started to move among the men, yelling at them, calling them names.

"Whattsa matta, Chuck? Can't you take it?"

"Lay off, Fred. I'm not coasting."

"The hell you're not. Step on the gas or maybe you won't be able to pay rent next month."

Chuck grabbed at twine, slipped it around a package.

Fred walked around the room, shouting at the men.

"Come on, come on, come on – "

Paul leaned toward Ralph and said, "I can't stand it. It's up to my neck already."

"Take it easy," Ralph said.

Paul pushed a package toward another man. Fred walked over and his fists were on his hips and he watched as Paul took another package from Ralph and marked it and then reached for another package.

"Nice and slow," Fred said. "No hurry at all. Just take your time."

Paul took a package and it slipped away from him and he grabbed for it and fell over it and his knee dented the cardboard and ripped it slightly.

"That's it," Fred said, "nice and slow and careful."

Paul whirled around, "How'd you like to go to hell?"

"You talking to me?" Fred said. He was smiling. The men stopped working and looked up.

"I'm not talking to your grandmother," Paul said.

Fred stepped in and socked Paul deep in the stomach.

Paul doubled up, and Fred bashed him with a left hook to the side of the face and a right to the eye. Paul went down. Fred reached down and picked him up by the hair and smashed a right to the eye. Paul went down. Fred reached down and picked him up by the hair and smashed a right to the jaw. Paul went down. Fred reached for him again. Blood poured from Paul's mouth.

Ralph stepped in between.

"That's all," he said.

Fred said, "Yeah? Move aside."

Ralph didn't move. "It's enough," he said.

The men crowded around. Some of them were pushing boxes and packages out of the way. A few of them helped Paul to his feet. Paul said, "I'm not done yet."

"You're goddam right you're not done yet," Fred said. "That's just a taste of it."

"Aw, break it up," one of the men said.

Another said, "Leave him alone, Fred."

Paul said, "I'm not afraid of him." But he was shivering, and wheezing, and he had a lot of pain and a lot of fright. Blood rushed from his nose and mouth.

"Give me room," Fred said. "Give me plenty of room."

Ralph stood between Fred and Paul.

"Get outta the way," Fred said. He was bent low, fighting stance, moving his feet, shuffling, his fists circling in front of his face.

"Cut it out," Ralph said. "It's all over. He's hurt."

"I'm all right," Paul said. "I'm not afraid of him."

"You gonna get outta my way, you son of a bitch?" Fred said. He stepped close to Ralph, held his right up and ready.

"Watch out, Ralph," said Paul.

Fred threw the right. Ralph took it on the side of the jaw. He fell back, landed against a pile of boxes. He got up fast. He pushed Paul out of the way. Paul tried to get back into the circle, but the men held him.

"Take a last look at this guy's pretty face," Fred said, pointing. "When I get through with him it'll be mush."

Ralph rushed, hammered a right between Fred's eyes. Fred blinked and threw up his fists. Ralph smashed his fists through the guard and Fred took a right to the mouth and another right to the side of the jaw. He drew his right arm back to deliver a chopping punch to the head and that left him open for a right to the eye and another right to the nose and a left to the same eye.

Breathing hard, Fred stepped back.

"Give it to him! Give it to him!" the men yelled.

Fred knew they were not yelling for him. He wondered who this bastard was. Already his head was full of pain. His nose felt as if someone had forced a lot of white-hot lead up there. His right eye had hammer-pain in it. But he knew that he had at least forty pounds on this fool and all he needed was one good opening.

He rushed. He threw a right and missed. He was wide with a left. He took two rights to the side of the face and a left to the nose. He was bleeding. He clinched and held hard and bashed rights to the kidney and lefts to the ribs and tried to butt Ralph in the face. Ralph got one fist free and brought it up to Fred's chin. The clinch was broken. Fred fell back. Ralph leaped at him and crashed a left to the chest and another to the jaw. Fred went down.

From the other rooms more men came running. They crowded about the circular space. They stood on packages and boxes. Everybody was yelling.

"Attaboy, Ralph!"

"Give it to him, Ralph!"

"Knock his goddam head off!"

"Give it to him!"

Fred was up. He came in slowly. Ralph didn't wait for

him. Ralph rushed and threw a right to the head. Fred was ready. He ducked, came in, clinched. Again he bashed the right to the kidney, and bored the left into the ribs. Pain bounced through Ralph, and for an instant his eyes were closed. And then Fred butted him. Fred's skull hit Ralph in the forehead. Ralph went down. Fred threw himself at Ralph and grabbed him in a stranglehold.

Ralph slid his hand up under Fred's arm and his fingers were spread wide. His fingers jabbed up fast. His forefinger went into Fred's bad eye. Fred screamed and let go and rolled over. Ralph rolled with him. Fred tried to crawl away. Ralph grabbed him by the neck and twisted him around and smashed a right to the nose. Blood squirted.

They rolled over, crashed into boxes. Fred grabbed Ralph in a crotch-hold and lifted him high, slammed him against a stack of cardboard boxes. Ralph got up slowly. Fred leaped at him, bent to apply another crotch-hold. And Ralph brought his knee up fast, and Fred's head snapped back.

"My God – break it up!" a man yelled.

"Let them finish it out," someone said.

Fred grabbed at a box and threw it at Ralph. Ralph ducked and the box whizzed above his head. He leaped at Fred. Grunting, bleeding thickly from nose and mouth, Fred threw a short right. It was wide. They went to the floor, twisting and kicking and squirming. Again Ralph jabbed his fingers up, and again one of his fingers went into Fred's eye. Fred screamed and threw his hands to his bad eye and fell away. Ralph rolled to the side and got up fast. Fred backed away. Ralph rushed him, fell into him and again they rolled over. Boxes toppled and crashed into them. They were up, swinging into each other. Fred was gasping. He was very bloody. He was falling. Ralph would not let him fall. Ralph lifted him with an uppercut.

Again Fred started to fall. And Ralph reached back with his right arm, brought his arm over his head. His fist came down and crashed against Fred's chin.

It was ended. Fred was unconscious.

Ralph didn't know that. A lot of men were closing in on him, to stop him. He didn't want to be stopped. He still had a lot to do. They weren't going to stop him. They were grabbing at his arms. He couldn't move his arms. He was kicking and writhing. He pulled one arm away and hit somebody in the chest. They were forcing him back. From somewhere a lot of red was coming down and it gleamed because it was wet and from where it came there was a lot of hurt, like a blade pushing in slowly. Even so, he still had a lot that he wanted to do and they ought to leave him alone.

The men pushed and dragged and pulled, and finally they had Ralph on the floor. They tried to talk to him.

"It's all done, all over. Take it easy."

"He don't even hear you, Joe."

Cold water came down and splashed into Ralph's face.

He blinked and sensed that his teeth were locked together. He closed his eyes. Opening them, he saw clearly, as if he had previously been looking through a curtain, and now the curtain was drawn away and he could see everything. He blinked again. He felt pain in his head, and then in his chest and his stomach and all over. Again he blinked.

"He's all right now," one of the men said.

"Another bucket of water."

"No, he's all right now," George said, pushing his way through the crowd. "Let me take care of him."

"You a friend of his?"

"Yeah," George said.

Ralph sat up, shaking his head slowly. He was gazing at the floor.

"You're all right now," George said.

Ralph nodded. George helped him to his feet.

"How do you feel?" one of the men said.

"I'm all right," Ralph said. He watched blood and saliva drip from his lips.

Men wearing starched white collars and neatly pressed dark suits came down the stairway. In their buttonholes they wore white flowers. They hurried down the steps, frowning and saying, "What's going on here?"

The men with dirty faces and calloused hands said nothing. As if they had rehearsed long and carefully for something like this, they stepped back and made a path. And down the path walked the starched collars and dark suits, fast and brisk and frowning down the path, to stop finally and stare at the form on the floor.

Fred was on his back and his arms were spread wide. His eyes were closed and puffed and dark green and purple. His nose was a mess. His lips were swollen and cut. There was blood on his clothing. There were thick drops of blood now drying on his shoes.

One of the starched collars put a hand to his face and murmured, "My God – "

Another starched collar turned to the dirty faces and said, "What do you call this?"

The dirty faces grinned. One of them let out a laugh.

"You're fired!"

"Am I?" the dirty face said. He clenched his fists and moved forward. "That's swell. Before I go I want to give you a little Christmas present."

"Now don't get excited – " the starched collar said.

Another starched collar was bending over Fred and saying, "We'd better get a doctor for this man."

From the street came the sound of the crowds and the carol singing and the jingling bells. And the voice of Santa Claus. The voices of children. The sound spun around over the heads of the pouring crowd on the seething street below the brightly colored lights and the cold grey sky.

Ken said, "I wish I was there to see it."

George looked at the floor and shook his head slowly. "I don't know," he said. "Somehow I'm sorry I saw it."

"What do you mean?" Ken said.

"I don't know."

"You must mean something," Ken said.

For a while they were quiet.

Then Ken said, "I think I know what you mean."

George kept shaking his head. "To see him like that. Just to see the guy like that. It got me kind of scared. If you had seen him. His eyes. I don't know – "

"Couldn't you stop him?" Ken said.

George shook his head. "Nobody wanted to stop him. And even when they did, it took about twelve of them to get him quiet."

Ken nodded slowly. "I remember once when we were kids, he – "

George said, "I remember a lot of times. Once he – "

They stopped. They looked at each other.

Ken said, "Christ Almighty."

They said nothing for a while.

George said, "They took this guy Fred to the hospital."

"What about Ralph?"

"He was fired."

Dippy walked in.

"Peace, brothers," he said.

"To hell with you," Ken said.

"Where's Ralph?" Dippy said.

George told him what happened earlier in the day.

Dippy rolled a cigarette and said, "What is this?"

Ralph sat on the edge of the bed, looking at the paper on

which he had put down some words. Maybe Ken would get an idea from the words. He really didn't care whether Ken got an idea or not. He wondered why he had put the words on paper. He was only going to tear up the paper anyway. He put the point of the pencil to his lips. Slowly he lowered it to the paper.

The door opened and Addie stood there.

Ralph looked up and saw her and said, "What do you want?"

Addie said, "Mom says you got in a fight and lost your job."

"That's right. Get the hell out of here."

"That's no way to talk to me."

"Get out."

"I come to tell him I'm sorry for him and he acts like this."

Evvie walked down the hall and into the room. Her face was glowing from the cold outside. She looked at Ralph and said, "What's this I hear about you?"

Ralph said, "If you heard about it already, why do you ask me?"

"You're a disgrace," Evvie said.

"Yeah," Addie said.

"All right," Ralph said, "the two of you – take a walk."

The two of them walked out of the room, talking loud as they went down the hall.

Mrs Creel came upstairs and into the room and said, "Let me see your hands. Maybe you ought to have a bandage over your knuckles."

"Mom, leave me alone, please."

"Don't tell me to leave you alone. If your knuckles are cut you should have a bandage on – "

"Will you please leave me alone, Mom?"

"I'll leave you alone if you promise to put the bandage on yourself. Good Lord in Heaven. I should think a young man would have sense enough not to get himself in a mess."

"All right, Mom, you told me all that before. Please leave me alone, will you?"

Mumbling, Mrs Creel walked out of the room and down the hall and downstairs. She started to yell at her husband. She told him to go upstairs and give his son a good talking-to. Mr Creel was very tired from a hard day's work and he wanted to be left alone. Finally he put down the paper and told her to shut up. Addie and Evvie joined in. The three of them kept yelling at him. Mr Creel went upstairs.

He walked into the room, closed the door.

Ralph looked up. "Hello, Pop."

"I heard you had some trouble today."

"Yeah."

"Somebody get tough?"

"Yeah." Ralph put his hand in his pocket and said, "They gave me the week's pay. Here." He held it out.

His father looked at the envelope and shook his head. "Keep it," he said.

"No, Pop. Take it."

"You keep it for yourself."

"Know any place where I can get another job?"

"I wish I did. I wish I could find something for you."

"Here, Pop, take the dough. Give it to Mom, for the house."

"No. You keep it for yourself."

"If you don't take it, I'll give it to Mom."

"No. I want you to keep it for yourself."

Ralph put the envelope back in his pocket. He looked at the floor.

Mr Creel turned slowly and walked out of the room. When he was downstairs he settled back in the sofa and took up the paper again. His wife came in from the kitchen and said, "Well, what did you tell him?"

"I told him plenty," Mr Creel said. "Now, for Christ's sake, will you let a man read the paper?"

There was nobody on the corner. Ralph walked into the candy store and bought a pack of cigarettes. He walked outside and stood on the corner. When the cigarette was smoked half-way he flipped it down and stepped on it. A few minutes later he lit another cigarette. He figured that the guys were over Ken's house. He didn't want to see the guys. He had a pain in the kidney. He had a pain deep in the stomach. He had a bad headache. In his mouth he had a pain. There was slicing pain in his hands and in his arms there was wrenching pain. He had not eaten supper and now he was hungry but he knew if food was put before him he would not be able to touch it. He wondered what he should do. He wondered if he should go home and go to bed. He wondered if he should go over to Ken's house. He wondered if he should take a walk. He wondered what the hell he should do.

Another cigarette. Two kids walked down the street, arguing. One of them told the other that he didn't know anything about basketball. It was very cold. The pain was throbbing. He put his hands in his pockets and slouched against the wall and looked at the street. The headache was leaving him but the pain in his kidney was getting worse. He wondered if he should see a doctor about the kidney. A kidney was nothing to monkey with. He took his hands out of his pockets and looked at his knuckles. He wondered if he should have listened to his mother and bandaged up his hands. His knuckles were pretty well torn up. Peroxide had foamed, and then he had painted the knuckles with Mercurochrome and maybe he ought to have a bandage. But maybe it was better to let the cold air hit the cuts. He kept his hands out of his pockets. Cold air rushed into the cuts and hurt. He wondered what he should do. His kidney was a little better now, but he had a headache again. He looked up and down the street. It was empty. A car went by slowly, filled with people who were making a lot of noise. Ralph looked at the car. He watched it glide up the street. He had a feeling that the car was going to turn around and come back to him and the people would tell him to come along. He wondered where they were going. He watched the car glide into the darkness up the street. He slouched against the wall, looking at the ground. He started to walk away from the corner. He walked to the park. He was at the lake. He was alone out there. It was very cold and very dark. He walked slowly around the lake. The pain was no longer hard and throbbing. It seemed to be melting away. He walked very slowly around the lake, looking at the still black water. Parts of the lake were frozen. The ice glittered, fused into cold sparks that stabbed into the blackness. Wind soared through the park and across the lake and hummed through the gnashed branches of the cold trees. Beyond the scribbling of a leafless bush two lights blinked. Lights from two lamps far across the park. The lights were vague yellow. He knew they were not really vague yellow. They were bright white. But he saw them as vague yellow. He saw them as vague yellow eyes, vague in the darkness. And as he looked at the eyes he could see the vague flow of yellow hair. He looked away from the bright white lights screened by the quiet cold bush. He walked slowly around the lake.

CHAPTER 12

It was three days after Christmas. Ken was alone in the house. His parents were still in Vineland. They were going to stay for another two weeks, or maybe three. Ken had sixty-seven cents to his name. He had borrowed twice from his married sister in West Philly and he wondered how he should approach her the third time. George had gone home the day before Christmas. George's father had said that it was Christmas time and he wanted his son to come home. Now Ken was alone in the house.

He sat at the piano. He dragged deep at his cigarette and placed it on top the piano and let his fingers come against the keys. He played slowly and lazily, missing a lot of notes. He looked outside. It was snowing. It had been snowing since early last night. With hate he looked at the cold and the snow. He thought of Florida. He turned around and looked at the clock on the mantel-piece. It was two in the afternoon. He socked a few chords and then he frowned and started to peck at the keys with one finger. He grabbed for a pencil on top the piano and there was none. He ran into the kitchen. Where the pots and pans were kept he found a short pencil. He grabbed at some wrapping paper. He ran back into the living room. Dippy was now there, on the sofa, eating celery.

"What's that?" Ken said.

"They call it celery."

"Where'd you get it?"

"From my house," Dippy said. "Want some?" He

reached into the inner pocket of his overcoat, and pulled out a few stalks of celery.

"Come in the kitchen," Ken said. "We'll eat it with salt."

In the kitchen they wet the celery to make the salt stay on. They chewed away at it.

Ken pointed to the window. "Look at the goddam snow," he said.

"It's pretty," Dippy said.

Ken went into the living room with his pencil and paper. At the piano he pecked at the keys and started to draw lines on the paper.

In the kitchen Dippy looked out the window, at the snow. It was an army. It was marching down a big hill. In the valley the enemy waited. In the white valley down there a big battle would take place. Down the big hill came the army of white soldiers. Down they came.

At the piano Ken was frowning and hitting the keys slowly.

The door opened. Ralph walked in.

"Listen to this," Ken said. He played a few bars.

"Let me hear that again," Ralph said.

Ken played it.

"Is that all?" Ralph said.

"I just started on it." Ken whirled around on the piano stool. He said, "Where you been keeping yourself?"

"Around."

"You ain't been here since a couple days before Christmas."

"I guess I just forgot to come over. I was over to see George."

"Didja have a nice Christmas?"

"Yeah," Ralph said. "My grandparents came down from Doylestown. My grandfather brought a few bottles of wine. My old man started to pack it away. He was funny. My mother got sore but she couldn't help laughing at him.

We were all laughing. Then my grandfather started in."
Ralph laughed. He said, "The old guy was pouring it down
fast and before he knew it he had a load on. He and my old
man got together and they were a couple of real com-
edians. My sister Evvie got sore because she had that
guy Mayhew up at the house. The floor manager. They're
gonna be engaged. My sister Evvie was telling my grandfather to behave himself. While she was yelling at him the
old guy fell asleep."

Ken laughed. He said, "Maybe this Mayhew can get
you a job."

"Maybe."

"What kind of guy is this Mayhew?"

"Sort of a wise guy," Ralph said. "But I guess he's all
right."

"Whadja get for Christmas?" Ken said.

Ralph said, "My parents gave me a couple shirts, my
sister Evvie gave me a tie, and Addie got me some
handkerchiefs." He had taken the week's pay from Blayner's and bought his father a hat, his mother a brooch,
Evvie a nail-polish set, Addie a bottle of perfume. After
that he had a buck and a half left over. He bought a
bracelet. He didn't put any card in the box. He didn't want
her to know he was sending her a Christmas present. He
just wanted her to have a bracelet for Christmas. He
mailed the package to an address seven houses from the
corner of a dark little street.

Ken was saying, "I sent my old man a marvelous
Christmas present. We got a gas bill. He's always getting
himself worked up about the gas bills. So I sent this one to
him in Vineland, and on it I put 'Merry Christmas.' I can
just see him burning."

George walked in, shaking snow from his coat and his
legs. He put his hand in his pocket and took out two one-
dollar bills and handed them to Ken.

"What's that for?" Ken said.

"Room and board."

"Get the hell out of here."

"Come on," George said, pushing the bills at him.

"Don't bother me," Ken said.

"You know you can use the dough," George said.

"All right, but I won't take it off you. You can lend it to me if you want to."

"Then I'll lend it to you," George said. He forced the money into Ken's hand.

Dippy came in from the kitchen.

"Tomorrow is Saturday," he said.

"That's wonderful," Ken said.

"We'll have a party," Dippy said.

"I got a good idea," Ken said. "Call up those broads who stood us up last time. When they come here we'll be waiting for them with clubs. We'll knock their brains out."

"That would be nice," George said.

"I'll get something entirely new," Dippy said.

He turned the pages of the telephone book. He saw a name, and he looked at the address.

"Got something?" Ken said.

"This looks exceptionally good," Dippy said.

George and Ken laughed.

Dippy dialed the number.

A girl got on the phone.

"Hello," she said.

"Hello," Dippy said.

"Who is this?"

"An old friend," Dippy said.

"Who?"

"Philip Wilkin."

"Who?"

"You know – Philip."

"I don't know any Philip."

"You've got a bad memory."

"Who did you say this was?"

"Philip Wilkin." Dippy took a quick glance at the address. He said, "Theresa Jones introduced us."

"Who's Theresa Jones?"

"Now I'm sure you've got a bad memory," Dippy said. "Theresa used to live on the next block from you, on Nedley Street."

"When did this happen?"

"About ten years ago, but I have never forgotten you."

"What?"

"I said that I have never forgotten you."

"What are you talking about?"

"I am a successful system engineer."

"What?"

"I would like to see you again," Dippy said.

"Say, listen here, if this is some smart aleck trying to play a joke on me, I'll – "

"I don't care for your attitude."

"You listen to me, you smart aleck you. I am a respectable widow and I have five grown children. My two sons are six feet tall and they weigh over two hundred pounds apiece and I'd just like to – "

Dippy banged the receiver down.

"She's a widow," he said. "Weighs two hundred pounds."

He turned the pages of the telephone book.

"Here's something," he said.

He dialed a number.

"Hello."

"Hello. This is Philip Wilkin."

"Who?"

"Philip Wilkin, an old friend."

"Yeah?"

"Of course. I met you at Gardenia Dancing Gardens, remember?"

"Listen, I never was at Gardenia Dancing Gardens in my whole life. What kind of bum do you think I am?"

"Now please," Dippy said. He cupped his hand over the mouthpiece and to his friends he said, "This is all arranged."

"Who is this?" the girl said.

"I told you. Philip Wilkin."

"I don't know any Philip Wilkin."

"Well, maybe I got the wrong party," Dippy said.

"Well?"

Dippy waited. Then he smoothed his grease-sleeked hair and he said softly, "You have a very nice voice."

"Thank you."

"I would like to meet you."

"You would?"

"Yes, I would like to meet you. I am in town for a short business trip. I am here for a convention of system engineers. Several of my associates are here with me. Would you like to have your friends meet my business associates? They are all system engineers."

"Listen, if you're such a big business man, how come you were at the Gardenia Dancing Gardens?"

"I'm in a big hurry," Dippy said. "I have an important appointment and I can't waste any time. I want you to bring yourself and three friends tomorrow night. We're having a big party."

"Where?"

Dippy gave her the address.

Then he said, "Now I want you to tell me definitely if you and your friends will come, so I can tell the caterer just how many places to set at the table."

"Why don't you meet us at my house?"

"I'm in a big hurry," Dippy said. "Are you coming to the party – yes or no?"

"Well – yes, but – "

Dippy banged the receiver down.

"It's all set," he said.

CHAPTER 13

On Saturday night, as Ralph arrived at Ken's house, he could see no lights inside. He wondered where the guys were. He wondered what had happened to the party. He rang the bell a few times and nobody answered. He stood in the street and looked upstairs. The windows up there were dark.

He walked toward Dippy's house.

It was very cold out. On the pavement the snow became a hard, shiny sliding-board of white. At the curb the snow was piled up high. In the streets the chains on automobile tires clanged and sparked as they struck against the sections of asphalt swept clean.

Cold, dry air swished into Ralph's mouth, and down into his lungs and up to his head. Inside he felt clear and light.

It was a quarter to twelve. Lenore, alone in the house, was in her bedroom. She was not tired. She didn't want to go to sleep. But there was nothing else to do. Earlier in the evening she had arrived home to find a note from Clarence, stating that he was going to the movies. She knew what he was going to do after the movies. He had to get it somehow. She knew he was paying for it. She got a kick out of that. He would be home tomorrow morning, miserable. She got a kick out of looking at the misery in his eyes.

She walked downstairs and into the kitchen. Behind the ice compartment in the icebox she had a hiding place for her own food. Nobody else in the house knew about it. This was the third hiding place. Dippy had ferreted the other two. The son of a bitch wouldn't find this one. She reached in and took out an oily-papered package of cold meat, and fixed herself a thick sandwich. She made herself two more sandwiches. She made some lemonade to drink with the sandwiches. She looked around the kitchen. There was cupcake in the bread box. She had that.

Returning to her bedroom, she stood in front of the mirror. Admiring herself, running her fingers through thick blonde hair, she played her tongue along her lips and wondered what she could do instead of going to bed. She scratched herself in the armpits, started to get undressed, and heard the front doorbell ringing.

Probably the mother had forgotten her key. To hell with the old hag. Let her stand out there in the cold. Let her freeze out there. The bell rang again. Lenore leaned her weight on one foot and put her hands on her hips and thought of how warm it was in the house and how cold it was out there. A third time the bell rang.

And then Lenore remembered that although they all had keys, the front door was not locked. She remembered that she had not locked it tonight. She wondered who was at the front door. The bell was not ringing now. Whoever it was must have gone away. But she wanted to know who had been ringing the bell.

She hurried downstairs, opened the front door. She saw him walking away.

"Hey!"

Ralph turned.

"Come here," Lenore said.

Ralph walked back to the house. He stood at the foot of the steps.

"What did you want?" Lenore said.

"Dippy ain't home, is he?"

"Come here," Lenore said. "Come on up. I want to close the door. It's cold standing here."

Ralph came up. He walked into the house. Lenore closed the door.

"Take off your coat," she said.

"Is Dippy here?"

"Not exactly," she said. "Take off your coat." She was looking him up and down.

"If he's not here I guess I'll be going," Ralph said. "Do you know where he went?"

"Sure."

"Where?"

"Why should I tell you?"

Ralph shrugged. He started toward the front door.

"Wait a minute," Lenore said.

"What do you want?"

"I want to talk to you. Come on in and take off your coat and sit down. What's the big hurry? You're not going anywhere."

"How do you know?"

"I know a lot of things," Lenore said.

"Yeah?"

Lenore put her hands on her hips and nodded and smiled.

They looked at each other.

Slowly Ralph took off his coat.

In the house it was nice and warm.

Lenore took his coat and carried it into the next room.

He told himself to get the hell out of here.

He sat on the sofa. She came in and sat down beside him. She had a pack of cigarettes.

"Smoke?"

"Thanks. I got my own."

They smoked. She crossed her legs. She was wearing a

silk dress that was rather tight. Underneath the dress she had on a brassiere and panties. She put her hand on her thigh and slowly pulled the dress up. He could see her soft, fat white flesh between the rolled garter and the edge of the dress.

"Do you think Dippy'll be home soon?" Ralph said, wondering why he was saying it, wondering why he wasn't getting out of here while the getting was good.

"I don't know when Dippy is coming home," Lenore said. "And I don't care," she added, very slowly. She turned and looked at him.

He gazed at the floor.

Her dress went up a little higher.

She stood up. "Wait here a minute. I'll be right down."

On the sofa Ralph told himself to get out and get out fast. But he sat there, waiting.

And then he heard her calling, "Come upstairs. I want to show you something."

He stood up. He went into the next room and grabbed his coat. He walked to the front door. He stood there, shifting the coat from one arm to the other.

The coat dropped to the floor.

He went upstairs.

He went into the room. It was dark, except for orange light from the hall.

She was leaning against the dresser, with her hands on her hips. Her lips were wet, and she was sliding her tongue over them again. And then she moved very slowly toward him. He took one step backward and stopped. She came nearer and he got a whiff of perfume. She came up close and put her fat arm around him and let it edge up to his neck. Her fingers played along the back of his neck and his ear and up into his hair. She put the other arm around his middle and pulled him to her. His head went down and she pushed her lips up and clamped them onto his lips and she smiled slowly as she felt his arms sliding around her and tightening. For a while they stood there, and she had his lips locked. Then she was kissing him all over the face. Then she had his lips again. She forced her tongue through his lips. She pulled him to her, and she went back and they were on the bed. She was kissing him and undressing him. She unbuttoned his shirt while he cupped his hand under one of her big breasts. She unhooked his suspender buttons and unbuttoned his pants and pulled them down and threw them on the floor. He started to roll away from her and she rolled on top of him and got hold of him again and put her lips on his.

His eyes were closed. She knew that she had him. She rolled over and took him with her. Then she sensed that he was trying to squirm away. She knew he was scared. But now he was on top of her. His arms were tight. He had a terrific grip. He was trying to let go but he couldn't. She pulled him tightly. She clamped her lips onto his lips. She pulled as hard as she could because she knew he was trying to get away and all she had to do was to let up for the slice of an instant and he would roll away. She didn't want to let this one get away. He was all right. He was better than the others. He had a terrific grip. He was scared now but he would get over it and she would see a lot of this one. She couldn't let him get away. She pulled him down and kept pulling hard and throwing herself up at him. He was still trying to get away. She couldn't let this one get away. Just then she felt his fingers sink into her arms, just above the elbows. It hurt. She thought he was trying to break her arms. She opened her eyes. She looked up at his face. She looked into his eyes. She became very frightened and breathed fast and hard. Her mouth was open and she wanted to yell but she couldn't get sound through her lips. And she couldn't stop looking at his eyes. He was hurting her now. He had a grip on her

that made the breath swish up past her lips, forced
her head back. And she was gasping. But her eyes were
open. She couldn't stop looking at his eyes. Then her
mouth was open very wide, and her teeth quivered and
her entire body quivered, because she was getting it with
more force and with more throb than she had ever gotten
it before. Her eyes were closed. Her teeth were locked. A
thin whistle stretched out as she breathed in. Then she
started to moan. And within the moaning, she smiled.
Now she had someone who gave it like a beast.

CHAPTER 14

Cracking an Indian Nut between his teeth, George walked into Ken's house. Outside, the Sunday afternoon offered very little sun.

Ken started to talk about Florida.

"So help me God, if I have to stay in this town another week I'll go out of my head. This time I'm set. I'm shooting down to Miami like a beaver. I'm getting in with the glace and the velvet."

Dippy walked in.

George and Ken looked at Dippy and started to laugh.

"Good morning, men," said Dippy.

George and Ken could not stop laughing. Dippy wondered what they were laughing at. He examined himself and discovered that his fly was open.

"What is this?" Dippy said. He buttoned his fly.

George pointed to the front window. "Look at all that snow."

Dippy said, "We should have a sled."

"What?" Ken said.

"A sled," Dippy said. "It's fine for sledding. I like to sled."

"Listen to him," Ken said.

Dippy said, "If I had a sled I would find the biggest hill. I'd go down real fast. I'd go down that hill a lot of times. I know a hill up in Germantown that some boy broke his neck on last year. That's how big the hill is. I'd like to have a big sled."

Ken stood at the bass section of the keyboard and hit a few chords.

Dippy said, "A sled is just what I'd like to have. If I had a sled I'd go right down the street. Look how the street goes down. I'd like to find a street that would just keep on going down. Do you think they have streets like that?"

"Like what?" George said, looking at the floor and thinking of all the things he didn't have.

"Just ignore him," Ken said, and hit another chord.

Dippy said, "A street that would keep on going down. Not a street. I mean a hill. I would get on my sled. I would go down the hill, and there would be a lot of ice so I would go real fast. I would break all records."

Ken turned away from the keyboard. He looked at Dippy. He said, "Suppose I showed you a hill like that. What would you do?"

"It has to be real icy and slippery," Dippy said.

"All right, it's real icy and slippery," Ken said. "Then what?"

"Then I'd go down on my sled."

"You'd just keep on coasting down the hill," Ken said.

"Real fast," Dippy said.

"Faster all the time," Ken said.

"Fine," Dippy said.

George looked up from the floor. He said, "How would you get up again?"

Dippy said, "Why do I have to go up again? The hill keeps on going down. I just keep on coasting down the hill."

"Coasting," Ken said.

"Better than climbing," Dippy said.

"A hill that just keeps on going down," Ken said. "Slide down, faster all the time."

"Faster and faster and faster," Dippy said.

"Where you gonna find a hill like that?" George said.

"You buy me a sled and I'll go look for one," Dippy said.

"There ain't any hills like that," Ken said.

"Are you positive about that?" Dippy said.

George and Ken laughed.

The door opened, and Ralph walked in. He was wearing a thick sweater over his grey flannel suit.

Ken looked at Ralph and said, "You look snakebitten."

Ralph said, "I left my overcoat at Dippy's house last night."

"That's right," Dippy said. "I saw it there."

"I went over to see if Dippy was there. I thought all you guys would be there. None of you were here when I came over."

"Didn't you hear about what happened?" Ken said.

Ralph shook his head.

They told him how the girls had stood them up and ruined their plans for the party.

Then Dippy was saying, "It's too bad that we couldn't have the party. I'll make some more calls. We'll have the party next week."

Ralph said, "Look, Dippy, will you get my overcoat?"

"Certainly," Dippy said.

"Will you get it for me soon? I'm cold walking around in this sweater."

"I'll go over and get it for you now," Dippy said.

"You don't have to make a special trip," Ralph said. "Later will do."

Ken said, "How come you left your overcoat in Dippy's house?"

Ralph shrugged. "I'm always doing things like that."

Dippy said, "When I came in I saw the coat on the floor."

"On the floor?" Ken said.

"Near the door," Dippy said.

Ken looked at Ralph and said, "How come?"

Ralph said, "I guess when I was waiting for Dippy I sort

of fell asleep. I guess I was in a fog when I got up. I didn't feel too good anyway."

"Yeah, but after you got outside and the cold air hit you, didn't you remember about the coat?" Ken said.

"No," Ralph said.

"It just seems queer," Ken said.

"I'll get the coat for you, Ralph," said Dippy.

"Leaving it on the floor," Ken was murmuring. "On the door near the door, and walking out of the house and it was cold last night, in spades."

Dippy looked at Ralph's sweater. He said, "I'll go over to my house and bring you your coat."

"You don't have to bother now," Ralph said.

"Don't be ridiculous," Dippy said. He put on his torn overcoat and walked out of the house.

It was a quarter to three in the afternoon. Lenore had just finished her breakfast. She was in the living room, on the sofa, looking at a new picture magazine dealing with night life in Hollywood and Manhattan.

Upstairs an argument was taking place between Clarence and his mother.

Lenore turned a page. She looked at the page and then she looked at her slippers. She looked at the edges of her pale orange satin pajamas. She put her hand under her knee. She ran her hand up along the satin that was tight and smooth against her thigh. She kept running her hand up and down.

A door slammed upstairs, and the mother was saying in a very loud voice, "I don't want to talk about it any more. Leave me alone. Leave me alone leave me alone leave me alone!"

Lenore turned a page and looked at the page and yelled, "Shut the hell up!"

Upstairs they were yelling and screaming. Doors were opening and slamming.

Lenore put her hand between her legs and slowly squeezed the soft smooth satin against her flesh.

Dippy came in.

"How do you do?" he said.

Lenore looked at a page and said, "Break a leg."

"Where is Ralph's overcoat?" Dippy said.

"What?"

"Last night I came in and I saw Ralph's overcoat on the floor, near the door. I put the coat on a chair in the other room." He pointed at the chair. There was no coat on the chair. He said, "Where is the coat?"

Lenore kept looking at the page. She said, "How should I know?"

"Tell me where you put the coat," Dippy said.

"What are you talking about?"

Dippy said, "I wish they would make less noise upstairs so I could hear what I'm saying."

Lenore said, "Listen, you. Get the hell out of here and stop annoying me."

"Where did you put the coat?" Dippy said.

"Take a walk."

"It's cold out," Dippy said. "It's real cold out. Ralph has no overcoat. He's wearing a sweater – "

"Now whaddya know about that?" Lenore murmured, turning a page and looking at the page.

"Tell me where you put the coat," Dippy said.

Lenore threw the magazine on the floor. She stood up. She yelled, "You get out of here and leave me alone! What do you mean by coming in here and accusing me of stealing overcoats! You go back and tell your friend that if he wants his overcoat he should come over here and get it himself. Go on back and tell him that. Go on. Go on back and tell him. Tell him that I told you to tell him."

"It's cold out," Dippy said.

"Good," Lenore said.

"What should I tell him?" Dippy said. "Say it slow this time."

"Tell him I said if he wants his overcoat he should come over himself and get it. Go on. Go tell him that."

Dippy walked to the door. He turned around. He looked at Lenore. He did not wonder why she wanted Ralph to come over for the coat. He knew only that it was very cold outside and that a sweater was not enough to keep the cold away. He wanted Ralph to have the coat. He walked out and hurried up the street, and over to Ken's house. Ralph was not there. Ken asked Dippy where he was going. Dippy did not answer. He was in a big hurry. He ran over to Ralph's house. Ralph came to the door. Dippy told him what Lenore had said.

Ralph looked at the floor. Then he looked at Dippy and he said, "Will you do something for me?"

"Of course," Dippy said.

Ralph said, "You go back to Lenore and tell her I'll be over for the coat. Tell her I'll be over in a little while – a few hours. And in the meantime, don't tell anyone about this."

Dippy ran back to the house and told Lenore what Ralph had said.

"Is that all he said?" Lenore murmured, looking at a page and smoothing her hand along the pale orange satin that was tight and smooth across her soft fatness.

Dippy said, "Certainly." He walked to the door.

"Where are you going?"

"Over to Ken's house."

"How long will you be there?"

"Until late tonight, I imagine," Dippy said.

"That's good."

"What?"

"Nothing."

Dippy walked out of the house. He started toward Ken's house. He was almost there when he stopped. He turned around. He was thinking about Lenore. He was thinking about what he knew about her. He was thinking about the time he had seen her get out of a convertible that had stopped in front of the house early one morning, and he was thinking about the time he had seen her coming out of a house a few blocks away, and a man came out and ran after her and they started to argue and he heard what they were saying and what they were calling each other.

He was thinking about those times, and other times. He was thinking about once when he had been coming home at five in the morning and he had seen Lenore and a man in front of the house. And he had sneaked around the alley and crawled up near so that he could hear what they were saying. Lenore was telling this man that if he knew what was good for him he better do what she told him, because she had enough on him to give him plenty of trouble. If this man knew what was good for him, he better do what she told him to do, and keep his mouth shut. Dippy was thinking of that. And he was thinking of how Lenore always explained to Clarence that she was going to see her sick sister. Dippy was remembering the nights, all the nights when Lenore was supposed to be at the sick sister's place, and he had seen her getting out of cars, walking down the street with a man, walking out of a house a few blocks away.

Thinking about Lenore, he was thinking about Ralph. He was thinking about Ralph and the overcoat. He was thinking about what Lenore had said, that he should go over and tell Ralph to come over for the coat himself. Thinking about that, he was remembering the time when Lenore had looked at Ralph, who was drunk and asleep on the couch, and he was remembering the way Lenore had looked at Ralph. He told himself there was no use thinking about the situation because there was nothing he could do about it. But he couldn't help feeling sorry for Ralph. He shrugged and resumed walking toward Ken's house. His lips moved and he was saying aloud to himself, "What is this?"

From upstairs there was a lot of noise. Doors were slamming. There was yelling and screaming.

In the living room, on the sofa, Lenore rested on her side, and slowly turned the pages of the picture magazine. She ran her other hand slowly down the soft smoothness of the satin that was tight and smooth against her flesh. She slowly smoothed her hand behind her, down along her spine and over her hip and down around the soft fatness, slowly smoothing her hand along the satin, over the softness.

Upstairs, Clarence was screaming.

Lenore looked upstairs and yelled, "Goddam it, shut up!"

The mother ran into a room and slammed the door.

Clarence followed, yelling and screaming.

Lenore yelled, "Bring me down my box of candy!" She smiled contentedly, knowing how it would end. It always ended with the two of them running out of the house.

The mother was yelling, "Leave me alone! Oh my God, Why don't he leave me alone?"

"And if I do leave you alone? Then what? Suppose I do just that? Suppose I leave you entirely alone?"

Lenore slid slowly off the sofa. She walked to the foot of the stairs. She yelled, "Tell her, Clarence, tell her!"

"Oh, God help me!" the mother was yelling. She came running downstairs, twisting her arms as she tried to get a coat on. She was sobbing and yelling. She nearly fell on her face. She did not look at Lenore. She ran out of the house.

Clarence raced downstairs. He was breathing fast and hard. He opened his mouth to say something and he choked and opened his mouth to yell and he choked again. Then he gasped, "Where did she go?"

Lenore put her hands on her hips and said, "How the hell should I know?"

Clarence put his face in his hands and shook his head.

Slowly Lenore turned her head to the side and looked at Clarence. Her mouth was open. Her tongue worked slowly around her lips, sliding back into her mouth to collect wetness and wetting her lips slowly. And she was saying, "Maybe you better go out and look for your mother. Maybe you better find her before she does something to herself."

"My God, what do you mean?"

"Maybe you better go out and look for her," Lenore said.

Clarence ran into the next room and grabbed his hat and coat. At the front door he buttoned the coat and pushed the hat low over his forehead. Then he ran back into the next room and opened a closet door and took out a muffler. He raced back into the living room. He was breathing very hard. He unbuttoned his coat. He wound the muffler around his neck. He buttoned the coat and ran out of the house.

Lenore walked upstairs. She took the box of candy downstairs. On the sofa she rested on her side and filled her mouth with candy and slowly turned the pages of the picture magazine. She looked outside, at the snow and the ice and the wind. She looked at all the cold outside. She smiled and reached for a big piece of candy.

CHAPTER 15

Hearing the feet scraping against the ice, Lenore looked out the window. She saw Ralph coming up the steps.

When he walked into the house she was slowly turning the pages of the picture magazine.

"I came to get my overcoat," he said.

She looked up slowly. She rolled slightly to one side. "Is that all you come to get?"

"Yeah."

"You sure about that?" she said.

"Yeah."

"Come here, you," she said. "Come over here to me."

"Nothing doing."

"Come here, I said."

"Not a chance. I came to get my overcoat."

"Then what?"

"Then I'm getting out of here."

"And then?"

"That's all," he said.

"Oh, you think so?" she said slowly. She was rolling slowly back and forth on the sofa, on her side, and where the satin curved big and round she smoothed her palm back and forth.

"Give me my overcoat," he said.

"What's the hurry?"

"I want my overcoat and I want to get out of here."

"What's the matter? Don't you like this house?"

"No."

"You seemed to like it well enough last night."

"Last night was last night," he said.

"Oh," she said, bringing her head back slowly, "so that's the way it is."

"Yeah."

"Well, it ain't that way at all, see?" Very slowly she got up off the sofa. Then she stepped fast up to him and her face came up close to his and she was saying, "It's altogether different from the way you think it is. You think I'll hand you your overcoat and you'll walk out and that's all there is to it. But it's not gonna be that easy. When I feel like telling you to walk out, then you'll walk out. But I don't feel like telling you to walk out. From now on you'll be around when I want you to be around."

"What are you talking about?" He stepped away from her.

She stepped toward him. "Maybe you're stupid," she said. "Maybe I gotta draw pictures for you."

"What?"

"You know what I'm talking about," she said.

"I don't know."

"Now go ahead and tell me you didn't know what you were doing last night."

"I knew what I was doing."

"You're damn right you knew what you were doing."

"Look, what do you want?"

She stepped away from him, to look him up and down. She put her hands on her hips. She said, "I want what you got. I've been looking for something like that for a long time. Now I got it. I got something that puts me on fire and then knocks me out. That's what I always wanted. You think I'm gonna let go of it? You think I'm gonna let it walk out the door? Try another think."

Ralph frowned. He shook his head a little, as though he didn't quite get the drift of all this. And he said, "Are you making plans?"

"They're all made already."

"Is that so?" he said. "Well, you can throw them out the window."

She smiled at the belligerency in his eyes. "You're cute," she said. "That's what gets me. I feel like pinching you. I feel like running out and buying you neckties. It's the first time I ever felt this way toward a man."

"Give me my overcoat and let me get out of here."

"Where will you go?"

"I don't know where I'll go."

Lenore nodded, as though this was the answer she had expected. "You bet your sweet life you don't know where you'll go. You don't know what you'll be doing tonight. Or tomorrow. Or the day after tomorrow. What are you? What do you do? You stand on the corner. You're one of the bums. You're thirty years old and what do you have?"

"Nothing."

"Is that what you want?"

"It gives me very little to worry about. I don't have to think about losing it. There's nothing to lose."

She nodded with emphasis, and it threw him off balance, because it was as though she agreed entirely. Abruptly her manner became soft, there was sympathy in it, there was an element of understanding. She walked toward the sofa and plumped herself into it and looked at the wall on the other side of the room.

"You and me have an awful lot in common," she said.

He didn't know what to do, or how to take it. He tried to detect strategy in this new mood she had suddenly assumed, but it impressed him as something genuine, as though she had no idea it was giving him that impression. He was forgetting about the overcoat, about the plan she had referred to. He was concentrating on watching her and waiting for what she would say next.

"We're a couple of people who live in hard times," she

said, continuing to look at the wall. "I'm older than you are and I can see these things a lot clearer. We give ourselves the idea we can do better than we're doing, and some days we get bright ideas and try to put them into play. But it's no go. You can't get off a ferris wheel when it keeps going around and around. I've been aching for a smart apartment and a yellow piano." Her fat arm indicated the dreary room. "Look what I got."

He pushed fingers into a trousers pocket and took out a pack of cigarettes. He put a cigarette in his mouth and gave one to Lenore and struck a match.

Lenore pulled a lot of smoke into her throat and let it out in jagged little clouds as she said, "What is it with us? It's trying to get things. We keep trying to get things. When we get them we develop all kinds of crazy schemes to hold on. Like the scheme I thought I'd work on you."

She laughed. She was laughing at herself. It was a little laugh, without much sound to it.

"You'll get a kick out of it," she said. "It strikes me funny, just thinking about it." She was still looking at the wall. "I was gonna tear my dress and raise a rumpus and claim rape."

"That was brilliant."

"Who said I was clever?"

Ralph walked across the room and sat down in a tattered chair. He blew smoke toward the floor. "I'm wondering where I'll be ten years from now."

"There's only one thing you can be sure of. You'll be ten years older."

"Maybe not even that," he said. "Maybe I won't even be alive."

"You expect to be hit by a truck?"

"It could happen."

"The world could blow up. That could happen, too."

He watched the smoke from his cigarette as it left his

lips and sprayed toward the floor. "You think a lot about these things?"

She shook her head. "Hardly ever. I couldn't tell you the last time I thought about it. The people I'm with ain't the kind of people who get me to thinking. Not that it bothers me. I'm glad I don't have the habit of thinking a lot. The people who think a lot these days are the ones you see jumping out of windows. In 1928 it was different. Jesus Christ, in 1928 I was married to a man worth three hundred thousand bucks. We had two Packards. A year later he took gas."

"What did you do?"

Lenore shrugged. "I went out looking for another man."

He hooked a leg over the side of the chair. "You don't believe in wasting time, do you?"

"Why waste it? There's only so much of it and no more. You, you've got ten years until you reach forty. Me, I've only got four. But I'm not kidding myself. I'm stuck in this house. Every time I tell Clarence I'm gonna pack up, he says he'll kill himself. He'd do it, too. The way he says it. Different from the way he says anything else. His voice goes way down and he just says it and walks away."

"Does that stop you from packing up?"

She nodded.

He leaned forward a little. "Where do I come in?"

"I just want you to be around," she said. "I want to see you once or twice a week."

"What else?"

"That's all. No strings."

He bit at the edge of his lip. Something jabbed deep into his mind. It was like a hook catching hold of the buried thoughts and bringing them to the surface. He heard himself saying, "I guess it's all a matter of what we can afford. I'm just a corner bum and all I can afford is a deal with no strings."

His head was lowered. His eyes were closed. In the
darkness under his eyelids he could see the shabby house
where Edna Daly lived. Edna was standing on the door-
step. For an instant he saw her clearly, then gradually she
faded, like something floating out of a dream. He opened
his eyes and saw the fat blonde on the sofa.

Lenore lifted a finger and beckoned to him. He moved
toward her.